I haven't heard from anyone for ten years; I guess it's all right to tell the story now.

Although others may argue the point, this is not a story about how I got here. It is simply a story of what I did before. I blame no one. It is one of the reasons that I do not talk. It would be pointless, and it would make no sense, and that is one of the reasons I am here.

With your kind indulgence, I will tell my story.

It was Mitch and Clyde who taught me not to talk. It was Maude Primm who taught me not to talk. It was The Laughing Man who taught me to laugh, and now they say that that is bad and that I do not understand the way things are and that I should change. I take no medication and request none.

My father came to see me once. He sat across the room in a chair and rubbed his thumb on his pocket watch and looked at me with big sad eyes. He said something to me that I could not hear. (They are under the impression that I can hear.) I looked at my father— he seemed so sad—and for no good reason. I got up and hooked my thumbs into my belt loops and walked around the room and laughed for him. He looked at me and did not join in.

It was The Thinking Man, The Singing Girl, my mother, and others who made me sad. And now I could see that it was people like that who were making my father sad. He once seemed so wise. Reverend Turner, Gloria Strong, Van Alexander and those kinds of people were making him sad, and I couldn't help him. I was afraid to look at him anymore, so I curled my legs up under my chin and turned my face to the wall and waited for him to close the door.

My earliest memories of my father and mother came from the time I was five or six years old. My mother used to tell people in my presence that I never cried, not even as a baby. She said that I was not demanding or moody. I was led to believe that it worried her for a few early years. She thought perhaps I was deaf or mute.

I once told my teacher at Woodmont Coves grade school that I could imagine an absolute nothingness. She looked puzzled and said, "Nothing? I don't think you should be doing that, how do you do it?"

I told her that I could imagine that the earth, stars, people and everything were not there, or here, or any-where.

Sometimes when I was playing in the school yard I

would see her standing inside the school building looking from the window at me.

I would sit under the bleachers in the Woodmont Coves school gym. The bleachers were portable, and there was room for a boy in his fourth year of grammar school. Moving around under there, I could watch what was happening on the portable stage on the other side of the gym.

The best thing I ever saw from under the bleachers was The Laughing Man. He was a local person from across the river, which gave him an air of import. But he was local.

The Laughing Man wore a suit made of a plaid material that was supposed to convey an impression of humor, but I never thought so. The only person I ever knew in a plaid suit had been phony and very unfunny. I had met him when I was three years old, and at four I was set in my prejudice about plaid suits.

 The Laughing Man was backstage, in the study hall of Woodmont Coves High School. He made sure the door to the makeshift dressing room was locked before he opened his black leatherette suitcase to prepare for the show. He removed some underwear and several pairs of socks from the top of his luggage and exposed a shiny bottle of good scotch whiskey and several neatly arranged bottles of assorted pills. Removing

the cap from one of the bottles, he took two of the small white pills and chased them with a liberal swallow of the warm scotch He ceremoniously replaced the tops of both bottles and sat down on one of the desk tops to smoke a cigarette and wait for a sign of the effect he desired. He wiped the perspiration from his brow and found it oily.

The Laughing Man had already set up his speakers on either side of the stage, he had checked his recorded music to make sure it was working, he had tested the row of buttons on a black metal base that was positioned near his feet at the bottom of his mike stand, and he knew that all was well with his equipment.

The Laughing Man never signed autographs and never greeted the public after one of his performances. In fact, it was the hardest part of his job, hiding from people who might want to talk to him after his shows. He was standing near the window that looked out toward the river, thinking of ways to escape the crowd yet another time, when a knock came on the study hall door. "Sir, we're ready for you, anytime."

The Laughing Man took one more long drink from the bottle of scotch, popped a breath mint into his mouth, locked his suitcase and took a deep breath before making his entrance.

What The Laughing Man did was entertain. He would start off into a song that was a kind of nonsense thing, and somewhere early in the song he would lose his composure, predispositioned I'm sure, and start laughing. It was mad, foolish, full-tilt laughter, and it was contagious. Every one of the 150 or so children and adults in the bleachers would begin to laugh with him. I would look toward the doors of the gym to see if the teachers were laughing, and they would be. I would look through the seats at the metal chairs in front of the portable stage where the elite of the community sat—and they would be laughing.

I was a laugher, too. Tears would roll down my cheeks from laughter. I would stomp my feet under the bleachers and laugh. I would pound my hands together in applauding laughter. I would close my eyes and shake my head in blind laughter. I would hold my stomach and indulge in painful laughter. The fat, red-faced man in the plaid suit would roll around the stage in professional laughter.

It was only a thirty-minute show. The Laughing Man would start a story of some sort and then break into laughter, and everyone would join in for another laugh. The Laughing Man's last bit was always "The Laughing Song," when he laughed in meter and rhyme. That was the best one of all—everybody knew when to laugh and how long.

Woodmont Coves was a low point in the geography of the area. The hills on either side of town formed a cup in which the buildings and houses sat. Looking down into the town from the hills, one got the impression that the brown and white buildings were struggling to get their heads above the hills and take a look at the wide world around them. There was a paint factory to employ the city dwellers and spacious, fertile farmlands beyond the hills. The economy of Woodmont Coves was a "one of everything" affair: one barber shop, one doctor, one bank, one fire truck and one overwhelming purpose—to survive. Although the basketball team did well in state competitions, there was little rivalry in the hearts of the people. The pace was slow. It seemed that people were walking around a stage as if waiting for something which no one dared talk about.

The Boo River swung around the little town on the south side. The river reflected the mood of the people: silent in winter, bustling in spring and lethargic in the quiet, easy summer.

My father, John Friend, was the town's medical doctor. His office was a little room in a wing of the house where he, my mother and I lived. At first I believed that he was hurting the people who came to see him. There would be crying and yelps of pain from the office in the wing of the house. I wondered if he would be caught and punished, and me as well.

The room was small and cluttered, with so little medical equipment you would not have recognized it as being a doctor's office were it not for the smell. I believed early that all medicine was made of the same basic component. It was a musty, depressing smell that was dominated by the odor coming from the hundreds of bottles of pills that were all over the place. For the most part they were samples that either came through the mail or were dropped off by traveling drug salesmen. My father would often rummage through them and hand them out to his patients with a prescription for more from Friedman's Pharmacy.

I think my father was, in his estimation, a failure as a doctor. He had given up early in his career. He would often say that there was little he could do for the really sick and that time would heal the others. Some of his patients were kept tranquilized or drunk. He would pour tonic into one of the plain bottles that he bought by the dozens and label it to be taken at intervals during the day. Many an old lady spent her last days in happy, drunken stupor.

My father also solved his problem with my mother, whatever it might have been, by addicting her to something that kept her face bloated and her disposition sentimentally happy. I never knew what it was that she took.

She made all of her own Christmas cards, painted silly little pictures, and was on the decorating committee of every social club in town. I was incapable of reaching her from where I was at that time.

She would implore my father to let me live my own life, which I considered a great psychological coup for my father, for it was he who had the original idea to let me live my own life. How he got my mother to think that it was her idea I'll never know. His mild protest on occasion gave an air of debate to the decision.

There were only thirty-three hundred people in Woodmont Coves. It was not easy, if nigh impossible, to keep anything from anybody. And so it was generally known that I was "curious" and that my father was agnostic. There were twelve churches in the area, and my father had said publicly and privately that he would come to church when they had settled on a single idea, which of course meant that my father never intended to go to church. He said that biology had no religion and that society's ills were self-inflicted and incurable, and he would have no part of anything so permanently sick. He did say once that he thought there was a good chance that a man could return to life as something else, as he had never been able to think that the soul and the body had any practical connection. In fact, he said it was a little absurd that so fine a thing as a mind should be connected to so fragile a thing as a human body. Natural selection could have made better use of the rock, he said.

I sold Cloverleaf salve to earn what little money I needed. I found that people would buy salve from a doctor's son. I would keep half of the dollar that I got for the salve and send the other fifty cents to the Cloverleaf Company.

It was not as pleasant a job as it might seem. I spent hours standing on the porches of the homes of sick people as they told me horrifying tales of their illnesses. It was because I was a doctor's son that they believed I would understand. I often gave them my best advice, which was to say, "Don't worry about it." My father would often say that those four words were his best medicine—don't worry about it.

Mitch and Clyde were the new winos. I met them when I was nineteen, a small, thin, bearded boy roaming the streets and the riverbanks of Woodmont Coves. I asked Clyde his name one day, and he said, "Clyde, that's all. When you see me coming or I hear you coming, you just say, 'Hello, Clyde,' and I'll know who you're talking to."

Mitch was more interesting than Clyde. That is to

say, he talked more. The trouble was that he never had any questions or answers in his talking. There were lots of stops and starts, but for the most part Mitch's talking was one big never-ending lecture to the world, thusly: "Now you take women, good morning ma'am. They's some good, and they's some bad, you can't always tell a woman—ha ha—so just let her be there. Whoa! It's time you took a look at that woman, ain't she sweet. Look-a-here. But never mind to be cool, just say, good morning ma'am."

On particularly slow days I sat and listened to about two hours of that, and I soon decided that it was not as enlightening and instructive as I first believed it to be. My best evaluation of the thing was that all of this talking was actually a scenario that was being played out in Mitch's head, and he was merely doing a running commentary on it.

Mitch and Clyde lived in a little alley between an auto parts store and a Cadillac dealership. They slept in a small shed between the Cadillac dealership and the auto parts store, up against the wall where it was warm in the winter from the heat of the building and cool in the summer from the dampness of the concrete blocks of the construction. Van Alexander, the tall, athletic, silver-haired man who owned the Cadillac dealership, was never harsh or impolite with us. More than once I caught him staring at me from a partially opened side door of the dealership. He would peer at me intently as if daydreaming. I would look back at him and he would snap his head as if he had just awakened.

Although it might have appalled Clyde and Mitch to know it, I think the man considered us watchdogs. The notion that we were lazy was considered an insult. And so the wine that was given us twice a week by the shop foreman was taken as a gesture of compassion and understanding. But we were watchdogs.

Mitch and Clyde never ventured very far from the dealership, except on the first of the month to pick up Clyde's military pension check at the post office. And on days of particularly pretty weather I would walk with them down Second Street because it had the most trees, and the liquor store was at the end on the right. Mitch bought a pint of real whiskey on one occasion— it made him sorrowfully sick—and for days afterward he could eat nothing. Our only other trips would be to the gym to see The Laughing Man whenever the posters announced that he would be performing.

I know now that what I liked about Mitch and Clyde was the celebration without conversation. We often had a couple of cans of the good chicken and dumplings that came in quart-sized containers with a warning that read: "Do not heat in can." We heated the cans anyway. Using a small container of Sterno sitting under a hubcap with a hole in the center, we warmed it somewhere beyond room temperature and ate with our forks, which we kept in our shirt pockets. It was a good, quiet celebration.

These were good times and did not subside in their festive air until Mitch started crying. He would look toward the heavens, and his face would have the saddest, most depressing look that I have ever seen. It was a hopeless moaning sound that Mitch made. He would shake his head in disbelief and, placing his face in his hands, he would sob until his body shook. After regaining his composure for a second, he would look toward the heavens again in anger and defiance. Then the melancholy would return, and he would burst into tears.

I once made a motion to comfort Mitch, but Clyde held out his hand toward me and shook his head in the negative. It was all I could do to keep from crying with Mitch. I somehow knew the feeling he had. Although I never succumbed to it, it bordered on my general disposition; and I felt helpless.

Of course, Mitch would recover from his crying and then would resume his monologue in an even more defiant tone: "Now, they's ways to do things, and they's ways that ain't. Ride that hoss cowboy and drive them horses off that screen. Shoot them wranglers and keep that white suit clean. It don't make no difference to watchers, do it while it's time to be done, and don't make no never mind to be cool, just say Hoo Hoo Hoo, Mornin' Ma'am!"

I later learned that if Mitch started crying, it was best that I take a walk. I would walk down Hill Avenue by the bus station, then back on the other side of the street and then back again if Mitch was still crying. I would walk quickly, as if I were going on some earnest errand. Sometimes I would find a newspaper at the bus station; and although Mitch and Clyde never read anything, I would read some unusual human interest story out loud, and they didn't seem to mind.

I once read them a story about a woman who killed her husband with a bow and arrow, tied him to the hood of her car and drove around the neighborhood until the police got her. I was pleased to hear Mitch include the episode in his monologue one day. He had a good time with it for a long time. I read him some other items of that nature, but he didn't pick up on them as he had the bow and arrow story.

I had a dream that my mother, father, Mitch, Clyde and I were all under the bleachers watching The Laughing Man. It was a grand performance, and I was so happy in my dream, as happy as I had ever been in my life. We were just at the end of "The Laughing Song" when Jesus walked up to where we were. He was laughing softly and quietly, as Jesus would, and I became angry; and even though I was nine years old again in the dream, I was very strong. My head was like a large block of steel. My shoulders and arms were big and muscular, and I had a pair of iron shoes on my square feet. I stood with my hands on my powerful hips and said, in a booming voice, "Get out, Jesus, you have no business here at our laughing show. This is for us." And I smiled a little knowing smile at my friends and my family. Jesus, frightened at my voice, turned and ran with his robe flying behind him, and we all laughed and laughed at the sight. My father slapped me on my powerful back and said something complimentary that I could not understand, but he was laughing when he said it. I awoke from the dream, afraid of Jesus and afraid for the fate of The Laughing Man.

 A judge, a jury and a good news-paperman would probably have found Miss Maude Primm guilty of murder, but the people of Woodmont Coves did not seem to think it necessary. Miss Primm was the thirty-five-year-old secretary of the seventy-five- year-old Dr. Friedman, who owned and operated Friedman's Pharmacy, the only pharmacy in Woodmont Coves.

It was generally known that Dr. Friedman had made out a will in which he had left everything he owned to Miss Primm. She was a tall, handsome lady who wore dark brown clothes and fashioned her hair in a bun at the back of her head. The high-collar dresses that she always wore gave her a matronly appearance.

Dr. John Friend had often said that drugs were an occupational hazard among pharmaceutical workers and doctors. Maude Primm's mood seemed to rise or subside to fit almost any social occasion. This led many to believe that she was making her wares available for her own needs and wants.

Dr. Friedman was a small, slim man who wore a gray mustache and silver-rimmed glasses, the glasses perched precariously on the end of his nose. If Dr. Friedman ever said anything that would alarm, insult, arouse or admonish anyone, it was never quoted in my presence. He stayed in the back room of the little phar-macy and bottled and packaged the prescriptions for Miss Primm, who dealt with the public on the six days a week that they were open for business. If it was any kind of romance that drew these two together in so dedicated a public service, it was a very proper one. Miss Primm lived in a small frame house on one of the better streets in Woodmont Coves, and Dr. Friedman lived in a small bachelor apartment above the pharmacy. The one occasion on which they might have been seen together would have been the performances by The Laughing Man, yet Dr. Friedman never came to the shows, which Miss Primm never missed.

Maude Primm would arrive at the pharmacy at seven in the morning and make a pot of coffee. She would walk across the street to the Main Street Diner and pick up a danish pastry in a small white bag and deliver the coffee and the danish to Dr. Friedman in his bachelor apartment above the pharmacy. On the morning of Dr. Friedman's death, Miss Primm was on time as usual. She walked to the head of the stairs and knocked on the doctor's door. "Dr. Friedman," she intoned, "your coffee and your danish." There was no reply, and so she repeated the announcement, her eyes searching the walls for dirty spots or cracks in the plaster. Since this routine had been going on for more than fifteen years, it was immediately alarming to Miss Primm when there was no reply. She tried the door and found it locked. Taking the key to the apartment from her purse, she let herself in and looked about the sparse furnishings of the first room. There was no one to be seen and nothing suggesting that anyone was there except a light from under the bathroom door. Miss Primm tried once more for a response. "Dr. Friedman, are you all right?" She heard a slight splash of water.

"Dr. Friedman, it's Maude. Are you okay?" The

reply was still a slight splashing of water. Miss Primm moved across the floor and pushed open the door to the bathroom. Dr. Friedman was sitting in the bathtub, staring at her wide-eyed and obviously alarmed. Miss Primm knew immediately what was wrong. She had been around sickness and accidents all her life, and she knew that Dr. Friedman had had a stroke. His left side was slouched over in the water, and the left side of his face had collapsed like a burst balloon. Miss Primm stood and looked at him for a minute as the doctor pleaded with her with his eyes. Miss Primm sat down on an old white metal stool and looked at the doctor for a minute. "Dr. Friedman, can you hear me?" The doctor pleaded with his eyes. "Dr. Friedman, can you move?" she asked. Dr. Friedman pleaded with his eyes. Maude Primm, dedicated servant and loyal secretary for over fifteen years, took a bite from the danish and sipped the coffee. Reaching into the tub of cool water, she pulled the drain plug and stood sipping the coffee as the water drained away from the frail body of Dr. Friedman. He pleaded with his eyes. When the water had drained away, Maude Primm replaced the plug and reached for the hot water faucet, turning it on full blast. "I'm sorry, my old friend. You would never recover from a stroke." She retreated from the small bathroom and locked the apartment door. On the way down to the pharmacy she took three of the small white pills which she had in her purse.

Jimmy Barrett, Woodmont Coves' chief of police, said later that Dr. Friedman was as pink as a lobster when he found him. It was considered one of those weird accidents that sometimes happens to old people, and Dr. Friedman was buried with the appreciative townspeople in full attendance.

Maude Primm bought a new car and started shopping for clothes in Middletown. She also started wearing her hair loose and dispensed medicine for some time until she sold the place and moved into Dr. Friedman's apartment.

Sometimes, when I had sold a few extra cans of salve, I would have a hamburger at the Main Street Diner in the evenings. I ordered them with everything. I would wait until the dinner crowd had gone and the place was about to close and then I would order my big treat for the week: hamburger, with everything, to go.

It was on one such night that I found Maude Primm there in a booth in the corner. When I came to the register to order, she waved at me, motioning me over for what I assumed to be a question. I walked to her booth and bowed slightly and said, "Miss Primm."

"Sit down," she said.

"Well, I was . . ."

"Sit down."

I sat down and felt uncomfortable without a shower, as I usually did with proper people. Maude Primm sat and looked at me for a minute. With her left hand she was pushing her breasts up into the cups of her bra. I would not have seen that had I been looking at her face, which I was not.

"You are a fine young man, James," she was saying. "I knew your father when he was a pre-med in Cincinnati. You are from a fine family."

"Thank you," I mumbled.

"There's more I want to tell you, James, but you know how these people are. Meet me in my apartment in half an hour. I think you'll find it interesting."

I knew her apartment well. I had been there on many errands from my father's office as a child. I also knew that it was there that she had murdered Dr. Friedman. I ordered a Coke and took it with me as I left the Main Street Diner.

I stood beyond the streetlight and waited for half an hour. Then I walked up the brown, unpainted stairs of the old apartment and down the hall to the left to where I knew Maude Primm was waiting. She later told me that she could see me from her window, waiting beyond the streetlight.

I tapped on the door with my fingers, afraid to knock, and it fell open into a dark blue mixture of light and shadow. I stood there, frightened for a moment, until I realized that Maude Primm had put a blue light bulb directly over her bed in the front room of the apartment and was lying there nude.

Although I was a small person in Maude Primm's bed—I was five ten and slim—I still believe that I learned the true meaning of incompatibility. I had heard the word and had read it in several places. Now Maude was moving one way and I was moving another; she was large and I was small; she was excited by the pills she was taking and I was lost in her dark blue bed. How she could be so far away from what was happening amazed me. She said little and I volunteered no conversation. We were failures as lovers, but in Woodmont Coves our options were minimal.

I guess our affair would have lasted longer had I not

met her in public one day at Givens' Hardware Store. I loved all of the gadgetry that Mr. Givens kept on hand, and he let me browse there as I pleased. I would sometimes help him unload one of the delivery trucks that brought his stock. Although I did not want a job, he would let me bring something to the counter after I had unloaded the truck. I would find an item that I thought was within reason for the labor I had done and hold it up for him to see. He would either put it in a bag or shake his head "no."

I had unloaded several large cases of paint that morning and was looking for a suitable reward when Maude Primm walked up behind me and said, "You never kiss me."

I turned to her in a mild state of shock and looked to see if anyone else had heard. "What did you say?" I whispered.

She replied in a too loud voice, "You never kiss me."

I turned back to the screwdrivers enclosed in see-through handles and realized that I had never kissed her. I turned back to her in a quiet anger that I did not like about myself and said, "No, I never did."

I picked up the screwdriver and waved it at Mr. Givens as I passed the counter. I didn't look for his customary nod of approval or disapproval. I kept walking, with my heart pounding, until I was back at the dealership with Mitch and Clyde. It seemed the only safe place after such an encounter, and it ended my affair with Maude Primm. She waved at me a few times to come sit with her at various places, but I avoided her.

Sometimes at night in my trailer I would wonder why I never kissed her. It seemed simple enough. I could not kiss a person who had killed another person.

Maude Primm was tremendously efficient. When she sold the pharmacy to a young pharmacist in Woodmont Coves, it was minus the following inventory:

Morphine
Codeine
Barbiturates
Birth control units

These were all safely locked in a small cupboard in Maude Primm's apartment. On more than one occasion when we were making love, she would tug at my beard and whisper, "It's a brave new world, James. It's a brave new world."

Maude Primm had also insisted that, as a lady who was above reproach, she would keep a key to the pharmacy and the locks would not be changed. The young man who bought the place had known her all his life, and so he agreed to the arrangement.

The Boo River turned south at Woodmont Coves. When the water rushed against the hill on the south side of town, it came roaring back to the banks of Woodmont Coves, thus creating the inlets that were to mark and name the town. There were good fishing holes in the coves, and it was a safe place to land a boat if you had a mind to get out of the main stream and build a fire or hunt for game. That was my notion of the thing as I considered the reasons for building a town there. There were more explicit reasons, of course, but to me it was a wide spot in the river.

The town would not have seemed so special had I not grown up there. It was quiet and adventurous at the same time. The trees made it special. I had heard that it was settled by a family who more or less worshiped trees. I remember hearing about them when I was a small boy.

They were strong, heavy-legged people with thick, reddish hair and an occasional mole that stood out against their red-tinged complexions. They were an obvious family of some *certain* heritage. Long before I was born the older ones had died or moved, and only the one daughter, Claudia Barnes, remained. In order to keep the large farm going, Claudia Barnes hired men from across the river to help her with the work. Now and then she would meet some young man that she liked especially well and start referring to him as her husband. She did this three times in a matter of a few years, and each of them lived with her and seemed happy. They also referred to Claudia Barnes as "my wife." I imagined it to be a major concern of the townspeople when Woodmont Coves was smaller, but time had passed, I was a growing boy, and there were stranger things to consider.

Claudia Barnes was not difficult to remember the second time you saw her. She was manly in appearance, with red hair and a wide, toothy face. I have heard it said that she occasionally had to shave the stubble from her chin because it was hairy. Her husbands were quiet, hardworking men who never said much about what they did or why they did it. One of them ran the farm, one ran the feed store, and another lived in a small apartment in town. As a small boy, I was not allowed to ask questions pertaining to the morals and individual reputations of my elders, but I did consider some to be questionable.

> Claudia Barnes, Claudia Barnes
> Has three husbands and a farm
> Raises hay and sells the hay
> Has three husbands by the way

That was a small poem that some of the children chanted in private, though I believed it to be written by an adult.

I would not speculate on the arrangement between Claudia Barnes and her three husbands. It was true that she had helped Woodmont Coves with a prominent farm, a feed store, and three hardworking men. The feed store was opened at a convenient crossroads and blossomed into what is now Woodmont Coves. Anyone desiring to move there, build a house and open a business would have to assume that Claudia Barnes would keep her three husbands, and so the matter was settled before it became an issue.

It should be noted here that the Barneses were very nice people. Gentlemen one and all, the husbands, and Claudia was always fair and honest in her dealings and had no public vices. There was talk that there were thriving vineyards on her farm, and none of the grapes nor their by-products ever left the farm as a matter of commerce. So it was assumed that Claudia would gather her three husbands about her and sip wine and sing songs and tell untellable tales.

Claudia had one very small husband who always came to see The Laughing Man. He considered himself as normal as the rest of us and laughed as hard and as often as he pleased. I would sometimes watch him to see if there were any traces of sadness or remorse about his situation, but he seemed altogether pleased with himself and sometimes stood to sing "The Laughing Song" just as many of us did.

If Claudia Barnes had any peculiarities, it would have been the fact that she seldom slept, or didn't sleep at the times and in the fashion that other people in Woodmont Coves did. There was a wide place in the road on the hill that led over to the river, and she would often park her car there, facing the road, and sit for hours into the night. Since no one wanted to approach her and inquire about her disposition or purpose, it could not be determined if she was sleeping or watching the road. I personally preferred to think that she was sleeping.

Claudia Barnes was watching for and cursing the drivers who hauled the pulpwood to the paper mill across the river. She, like her ancestors, loved trees, and she feared that all of the chopping and cutting of them for the paper mill would one day leave the countryside around Woodmont Coves bleak and bare.

It was a circus of vehicles that hauled the pulpwood. There were nice, new modern trucks, station wagons with the bodies cut away and some that were referred to as skeeterbugs. These were old cars of almost every make that had been cut down to the bare necessities for hauling the wood. The skeeterbugs were often without tops, fenders or windshields. Sometimes the right front seat would be removed in order to haul more pulpwood. Anyone wanting to sell pulpwood to the mill simply cut the wood into manageable lengths to suit the paper mill and got it to the site as best they could. Many farmers and poor families supplemented their incomes by cutting the trees on their property and fashioning a makeshift method of transportation.

The woodcutting was done in such a haphazard fashion and with such little regard for future ecology that it was shameful and wasteful in the eyes of Claudia Barnes. She loved trees in a way that some people would consider strange. As a young girl she could sometimes be seen in the forest hugging a tree, kissing it, and talking to it. Her love for trees was one reason for her choice of men. She wanted her men to be hard and strong and muscular, so she chose them from among the hardworking farmhands.

Among all her other idiosyncrasies, Claudia Barnes considered herself a witch. That is to say, she believed that she had the power to change events, cause things to happen and put curses on her adversaries. So she sat at the wheel of her car, lights out, motionless, and watched for the trucks and the skeeterbugs to go by with the day's supply of pulpwood for the mill across the river. She sat with lower lip tucked in behind her upper teeth and waited. When a truck or skeeterbug passed, hauling her precious trees to slaughter, she would murmur, "A curse on you, a curse on you, your life will change for the worse, tragedy will befall you." Then, placing her hand across the flat of her crotch, she would repeat in a shouting whisper, "A curse, a curse, a curse!" Then she would jerk herself upward by the crotch in a ritual that she had invented to bring vulgar and practical action to the spell.

It is unlikely that Claudia Barnes would have spent her nights in such a fashion had the curse not worked the second time she tried it.

Joe Louden had just passed Claudia Barnes, throwing a beer can into the roadside bushes. When he grasped the steering wheel of the old skeeterbug to use it as leverage to get a more comfortable position in the old seat, he was surprised to find that the wheel had come off the shaft and that he was holding it in his hands as the old rig, with an enormous load of pulpwood, headed uncontrollably into a pile of rocks and trees at the bottom of Hill Road. Joe Louden was aware that he had a scalding bitter taste in his mouth just before he died.

Claudia Barnes saw Chief of Police Jimmy Barrett go by with sirens blaring and lights flashing. She started up her car and followed him at a leisurely pace down Hill Road toward the river. It was there, with Jimmy Barrett's police spotlight shining, that she saw one of the most beautiful sights she had ever seen. The skeeterbug had crashed into a rock at the bottom of the hill, and Joe Louden's body was skewered on the steering shaft like a frankfurter at a picnic. The wiring on the steering shaft had been shoved toward the floorboard of the skeeterbug in the crash, and as the young man's body convulsed in death throes, the horn would occasionally sound. It was an eerie scene that she watched. Jimmy Barrett stood in a mild state of shock, and he would jump and let out a small cry as the jerking body caused the horn to blow every few seconds. Beep! Beep! Beep!

When Claudia Barnes heard the ambulance sirens coming up the other side of Hill Road, she turned her car and slowly drove back to her watch. She felt between her legs and was surprised to find that she had urinated.

Van Alexander had a son, Willie. He was a small, bull-like young man of twenty years, and I often wondered if his father knew, cared or discussed his obvious problem. (If, in fact, either of them considered it a problem.) The most memorable thing about Willie Alexander was his stubble of beard. He never had a beard as such, yet he was never clean-shaven. I often wondered how he kept it looking so even in appearance. I found out about Willie Alexander's homosexuality when I was thirteen years old.

Jimmy Barker and I were playing in an old abandoned house near the huge coal pile just across the river when the incident took place. Jimmy was a brave and loud young man whose behavior contrasted with my own quiet outward manner, even though I was imaginative and usually laid the rules for the games we played and the fantasies we enjoyed. On this particular day I had explained to Jimmy that we were defending the old abandoned house from pirates who had stashed gold there after boating up the river. We had made swords from pieces of wood and some nails that we had found.

We were running through the house to defend the north wall when we saw Willie Alexander. He was sitting on an old wooden chair with a shotgun across his knees. The house was bare of furniture except for the chair, and Willie's voice echoed around the bare walls as he said, "Stop there, stop there!"

Jimmy and I froze in our tracks because we had been told not to play in the old house and, in fact, not to cross the river to play. When Jimmy recognized the man in the chair as being Willie Alexander, he said, "Hi."

Willie said, "Don't either of you move at all. I got a loaded shotgun here."

Jimmy said, "We wudn't doing anything."

Willie said, "Just don't move or go anywhere, I don't care what you're doing."

I started to run, but Willie stomped his foot on the floor and said, "I told you not to move! Don't you know I got a loaded gun here?" His voice was trembling. When I realized that he was frightened, I became afraid, too.

Jimmy repeated his plea. "We wudn't doing nothen."

Willie pointed the gun at us and said, "You boys do what I say, and I won't shoot, okay?"

I shook my head up and down. I suppose Jimmy was shaking his head, too, although I was afraid to look. Willie tilted the chair back a little and said, in an almost crying voice, "You boys take off your pants."

Willie started crying and screamed at us, "I said take off your pants. Just take 'em off like I said before something happens."

I looked at Jimmy then, and he was about to cry, and that frightened me even more. So I shook my head for Jimmy to do as he was told and started unbuttoning my own pants at the same time. We dropped our pants down around our ankles and stood there nude from the waist down. Willie leaned even farther back in his chair and stared at us. Jimmy and I were not looking at him now. We had turned our heads more to the wall and only stole quick glances at Willie, who was almost smiling now. He leaned forward in the chair and rested the legs on the floor and said in a quiet, friendly voice, "Now you boys like me, don't you?"

"No," said Jimmy in a matter-of-fact voice. I am sure it was not what Willie wanted to hear, but then young boys are not given to lying when confronted by a man with a shotgun.

I don't remember how long we stood there. It was the first time in my life that I remembered sweating without exertion of some kind. Willie rocked in the chair, and Jimmy and I stared at the floor. After what seemed like a long afternoon Willie said, "Put your clothes on and get out of here." We ran across the railroad bridge that we had used to cross the river and didn't even listen for a train as we usually did. We never told anyone about the experience for fear that we would be scolded for crossing the bridge and playing on the other side of the river.

The only other time we ever encountered Willie Alexander as children was the time when we were fishing and he and some other young boys threw rocks at us until they drove us away from the water.

I would sometimes see Willie driving around town with some young boys in the car with him, and I wondered what they had been doing or were going to do, and it gave me a creepy feeling.

After I graduated from Woodmont Coves High School, my mother and father agreed to let me move into the trailer park on River Road at the edge of town. I had to use the laundromat on Hill Avenue, a block away, and it was there that I would meet my mother. She came there to wash linen in the big commercial washer that would hold heavy loads of laundry. My father demanded clean linen almost every day, as he was very particular about cleanliness. In fact, I often suspected that my father had an inordinate fear of germs. It was well known in Woodmont Coves that he would use no rest room other than his own. My father was a familiar figure in town, and it was taken for granted that you might see him anywhere, outside any social function or business place, urinating on someone's whitewall tires. The fact that he was a doctor, or maybe because he paid his bills, excused him from any proper place of relief.

My mother would find me in the laundromat and come to embrace me. Although I would often be wearing blue jeans and a T-shirt, she would straighten my nonexistent collar and inquire as to how I had been. I would assure her that I was fine, and she would ask about her letter. She loved letters. She would say that they were easier to digest than passing conversation. They were a comfort to her, and she could read them at will. And so it was that I lived a few blocks away and wrote and mailed my mother a letter like the following one every week:

Dearest Mother,

I was thinking of you at exactly 9 P.M., so I got my pen and paper to report on my activities for the week. I know that you are overworked these past few days because of your duties on the table decorations for the Strawberry Festival reception. I only hope you know how important your work is to the many fine people who benefit from the proceeds of the festival. The very heart and nature of the good people of the town are exemplified in your untiring and generous work on this committee. I have no doubt that this will be the biggest and most successful Strawberry Festival in the history of Woodmont Coves, and I can assure you that your contribution of time and talent for this reception will be the focal point of interest and inspiration for all of the other activities to follow.

Yes, I am beginning to understand why you wanted me to live my own life. Every day I see my way to a clearer understanding of what life is all about. I see now that it takes dedication and purpose to succeed in this world, and I am sure that any day I will find my niche and begin a career of some great merit and purpose. It is you, Mother, and Father who have given me this opportunity, and I curse the notion that I would be unappreciative of your sacrifice and direction. I know the burdens of parenthood are awesome, but I hope that you will one day stand in proud—no—glorious applause of your humble son's accomplishments. You have done your duty tenfold, and I can assure you that no word of thanks will pass my lips if it does not consider the mention of hard work and sacrifice that you have made. On any such occasion I will buy a blue suit and a maroon tie, which, as you have pointed out, is my father's best complement of dress.

If I am to succeed in my quest for acceptance, dear Mother, I must be at my rest. I bid you good evening and sweet dreams. Sleep in the satisfaction that you have done your all and have given full measure to your responsibility as a citizen and a mother.

With love and warmest regards,

Your loving son, James

Reverend Bill Turner had no sooner stepped past me onto the porch when my father spoke from the door of his office. "How do you feel, Reverend Turner?"

Reverend Turner, an ill-proportioned elderly gentleman with thin, white hair, walked into the office, stood thoughtfully for a minute, and said, "Dr. Friend, I have come to talk to you about a matter that concerns the spiritual health of this community. I do hope you will not mind my alluding to the practical nature of your work."

"Not at all," my father replied. "Have a seat."

Reverend Turner lowered himself to the cane chair next to my father's desk.

"Dr. Friend, I know you to be a practical and wise man. Even though I disagree with you on matters of theology, I still believe you to be in possession of a good and private mind. I will get right to the point. While I would not, for the sake of rumor, consult a psychiatrist, I do believe that I am in need of some professional help. I am losing my faith in the Lord."

"Go on," my father said.

Reverend Turner stood. He stared at the ceiling, then gripped his head in his hands.

"Go on? I just told you that I am losing my faith in the Lord, and you say go on. Don't you know the meaning of what I have just said? I am in charge of the largest church and the most influential congregation in the eastern conference, and you say go on. I am on the verge of madness."

My father had Reverend Turner take a tranquilizer. Then he took his stethoscope from off the hat rack in the office and asked him to take off his shirt. My father examined the preacher for almost ten minutes before announcing, "Reverend, I think what we have here is a very sound body and a slightly disturbed mental attitude."

It was surprising to see that Reverend Turner had

calmed to the extent that he had. He buttoned his shirt and spoke to my father in an altogether different tone of voice.

"Dr. Friend, what are your recommendations for the malady that I face?"

My father rubbed the face of his pocket watch with his thumb and said, "Reverend Turner, as you know I am barred from expressing a religious opinion on the basis of my profession. If I believed every word of the New Testament, my practice would be blasphemous."

Reverend Turner, who was calm now, said, "Now, Dr. Friend, I don't believe I would go that far."

My father waved away his objection to his philosophy and continued. "Now, Reverend, what you will have to do is practice your religion much as I practice my medicine. If you think you are losing your faith, then you will just have to operate as if you still had it. That is to say, you will have to do all of the things that you did when you had faith, and have faith that no one will be the wiser. You have admonished your congregation about their lack of faith on many occasions; perhaps you have been visited with doubt as a test of your own ability to deal with it. I would suggest that faith is nothing more than the exercise of good will and hard work. If you lose a spiritual faith, then you can work twice as hard on a practical one. Do good, do better, work harder, and soon you shall see that you are not the recipient of faith but perhaps the distributor."

Reverend Turner suddenly fell on one knee and, facing the ceiling of the little room, said, "Oh, Lord, bless this man, thy servant, this wayward soul who in time will return to the fold. Bless this kind sinner who has directed thy church and its leader to an even greater understanding of its mission. Bless this . . ."

My father tapped him on the shoulder and said, "I will send you a bill for fifty dollars for a complete physical examination, and that will be blessing enough if you pay it."

Reverend Turner rose to his feet and shook my father's hand. "I thank you, sir, for your trouble and your kindness."

My father straightened the tie of the preacher and said, in a very confidential tone, "God bless you, Bill."

 Although John Friend dismissed the question surrounding the affair as being academic, many of us in Woodmont Coves knew that Joe Morgan had killed his wife. Joe was of such stern disposition that few people knew him well. He lived on a small farm eight miles outside of town on River Road and seldom ventured into town for any occasion other than a few supplies. The supplies included a good deal of sugar, and this purchase led some to believe that he made his own whiskey, which indeed he did.

Joe was sitting on the front porch of his small wooden house, and he could hear his wife crying and praying in the bedroom inside. Joe was drinking some of his own whiskey and smoking a Camel. He got up from the steps of the porch and walked along the little dirt road that led to the place, out of hearing distance of the praying and the crying. He stood and looked at the smooth, easy flow of the river past his farm and dwelled on the peace that could abide there if it were not for the anguish of his wife, who was dying of cancer.

An old rooster scratched and strutted his way across the little dirt road, and Joe Morgan looked at it in envy. He wondered why the rooster did not have cancer. He did not ask much of this life, and he had decided as a small boy that he would not indulge in the petty conversations about its meaning and the origin and end of it. Things were as they were, and he was content to be clothed and fed. Joe Morgan's hunting, fishing and drinking kept him entertained. The stalking of game or the outsmarting of the fish in the river was his challenge. He could feel his heart going a little faster and could feel the sense of elation at catching or killing something.

The whiskey running clear and smooth through his veins raised his spirits, and he placed his hands in his back pockets and stretched to his full height as he took the fresh country air into his lungs. Out of hearing distance of the crying and praying of his wife, he made the reality of it go away with another, and still another, drink from the large canning jar of moonshine.

Mrs. Joe Morgan had been a melancholy sort all her life. Her father had been made of the same strong, stern stuff as her husband, and it was through these two hunting and drinking together that she came to marry Joe Morgan. Her first two children had grown and moved away to the big industrial cities, and her third had died at birth. Now she lay dying, and her husband let her know that he considered it her fault that she had come to such a mysterious end. Cancer frightened Joe Morgan. He somehow had the notion that it was visited upon the weak and the sinful; he also entertained the thought that a person could do something privately indecent and bring cancer upon himself.

Well, Mrs. Joe Morgan was beyond conversation now, and her husband knew that it was only a matter of a few days. Dr. Friend had given a prescription for some powerful painkilling drugs to Joe Morgan when he plainly told him that his wife had but a few weeks to live. Joe Morgan had had the prescription filled once. When his wife had taken nearly all of them in a matter of a few days, he had failed to return to the pharmacy for more.

Although he had thought of it before, it was suddenly clear to him as to what he must do. He turned on his heel and walked back toward the house at a brisk pace. His heart was pounding with the excitement that he had experienced on other such missions. His other prey had been much different, but he knew it would soon be over and that the peace and quiet of the country would return in a short time.

Walking into the kitchen at the front of the house, Joe Morgan reached into a pile of dirty clothes and blankets damp with mildew and extracted a pillow. He walked toward the small bedroom where his wife lay moaning. Standing at the door of the bedroom, he could almost hear the music playing. Boom! Boom! Boom! He walked to the bedside of his wife and placed the pillow squarely over her face and waited for her to die. Boom! Boom! Boom! the music played. Suddenly Joe Morgan was thrown straightaway from the bed onto the floor. "My God!" he screamed. "What's here?" He was shocked at the degree of strength of his frail wife. How could she be so strong? He rushed back to the bed and held the pillow over her wobbling head, held on with all of his strength as the woman kicked and tried to scream. The music was louder now. Boom! Boom! Boom! Then he felt something warm and liquid running from around the edge of the pillow across his hands. There was absolute silence in the room now, and Joe Morgan saw the blood and let out a scream so loud that it stopped his heart for an instant; he slumped unconscious to the floor of the little bedroom as the rooster crowed in the distance, and the cool, clear water of the river rippled across the rocks toward Woodmont Coves.

Dr. Friend signed the death certificate, which read: "Cause of death: Cancer, complicated by pulmonary hemorrhage."

Joe Morgan stood on the back porch of his little wooden house and cleaned his fingernails as he watched his wife's bedclothes burn in the backyard. He was still taking occasional sips from his canning jar as he wielded his hunting knife expertly. He would not have been so calm had he known that it was not dirt that he removed from under his nails.

The Strawberry Festival came to Woodmont Coves. It came in the form of paper strawberries, plastic strawberries, balloon strawberries, and water paint strawberries on the windows and shop doors all over town.

The weatherproof strawberries that adorned the sides of buildings, swung from utility poles as banners, and caught the eye everywhere fascinated me. Each of the big red berries carried a silent, subtle message. There would be strange, interesting people in town for a week. There would be lights in unusual places far into the night. There would be a mingling of cultures that were almost exactly opposite; world-wise travelers working side by side with small-town innocents. Merchants would be opening earlier and closing later to make more of the money that would be available during the festival. Farm boys would be selling their livestock, which had been fed and fattened for this occasion, and frugal parents would be digging into their pockets for extra money for the weeklong activities.

The Strawberry Festival brought drama and excitement to Woodmont Coves. A Ferris wheel could fall, rain was an ever-present danger to so large an outdoor activity, and law enforcement officials would squint their eyes and hold fast to weapons in fear of a manifestation of their distrust of the carnival people. Old men at the courthouse told thrilling stories of past Strawberry Festivals, and many of them closed their narratives by saying, "Mark my word."

My mother must have belonged to six or seven different committees. She was in on decorations, judged the ugly man contest, prepared food for sponsors' parties, made decorations, and was opinionated about every other movement or idea. Her exhausting, busy martyrdom was bewildering to watch. There were others like her, but my mother was the one who was always ready, always available, always tired.

I was asked to move from my little trailer for a week.

It was an arrangement that I had made with the old lady who owned it. When the Strawberry Festival came to town, rooms were scarce, and the ones that were available went for a premium price. It was agreed that I would move out for a week to make way for a very high-priced tenant who owned one of the Ferris wheels at the little carnival that was set up in the school athletic field every year.

I took my few belongings and stored them in a small shed behind my father's house. I changed into my best corduroy jeans and donned a T-shirt with a big red strawberry on the front. This done, I was ready for a week of festivities.

There would be parades, horse shows, a beauty contest, and a tractor contest to determine who had the best and most powerful tractor. One of the big attractions was a man sitting on a board over a huge tub of water. If you could hit a target with a ball, the man would fall into the water. I was mainly interested in the carnival side of things.

I had saved eighteen dollars for the festival, and I would use the money to entertain myself at the carnival grounds. There was a machine that I especially liked to play. It was a crane that operated inside a four-foot-square glass cage. If one maneuvered the crane bucket correctly, it would pick up an assortment of small items. I had spent most of my money the year before trying for a pocketknife and had almost gotten it a couple of times before it slipped from the bucket of the crane and fell back into the pile. It was a pretty four-bladed knife with a gold star embedded in the dark-brown wooden handle. It would have made a nice thing to have.

I went to the bus station to find something to read. I found a paperback Western lying on a bench. It was Louis L'Amour's *Under the Sweetwater Rim*. I put the book in my back pocket and walked up to see Clyde and Mitch at the Cadillac dealership. Mitch was doing a monologue on strawberries: "Strawberries ain't never done nothing for nobody no time, I say, hear now get up and after 'em while the sun shines. Wouldn't do to go being cool about it no way, it comes and goes and one is enough of a time if you go when the gooses ain't lookin'. Look out now, whoa here, say Hoo Hoo howdy."

Clyde was making some insoles for his shoes. There was a big hole in the bottom of the right shoe, and Clyde neatly folded some newspaper to fit in the bottom. It would last a week or so if it didn't rain. I sat down to read the paperback and fell asleep with my back against the warm brick wall and my arm propped on a concrete block.

L'Amour's characters had run into a burned, destroyed wagon train on the first page of the Western, and so it was that I dreamed that my father, Mitch, Clyde, my mother, Maude Primm and I were standing under the burned frame of the building where the bleachers of the school gym used to be. The school had been gutted by fire. I stood with my broad, square shoulders, my ironclad square feet, and looked across to where the stage had been. I was trying to assure my friends and family that it could be rebuilt and that The Laughing Man would return. In a wisp of smoke I saw the figure of Jesus appear. He looked across to where the six of us were standing and smiled a smile that I took to be vindictive. I turned to see if any of the others had seen him. They stood silent and expressionless and waited for me to lead them somewhere. I shuddered and awoke.

I hated the Strawberry Festival. I realized it when I was awake. I looked down at my chest at the huge red strawberry on my T-shirt. I hated the shirt, I hated the man who was in my trailer making love to the big fat woman who ran the milk bottle game, and I hated myself for getting involved in the whole affair with my good jeans and my strawberry T-shirt. I picked up the bottom of the T-shirt, pulled it away from my stomach and spat on it.

Clyde was watching me, and he sighed and shook his head. Then he stood and put his hands in his back pockets and stretched. Mitch ceased his monologue for a few seconds because we both took Clyde's actions as a sign of adventure.

Clyde walked out to the street and looked both ways at the traffic that was beginning to pick up in the late afternoon. He always did this before going out on the sidewalk. We never knew why. Clyde turned to Mitch and me and waved at us to join him on the sidewalk. Mitch rolled over on his stomach and came to his feet by way of his hands and knees; it was a thing he did often.

Clyde and I led the way as Mitch shuffled along behind us doing his strawberry monologue. We walked down Hill Avenue at a slow, deliberate pace, not talking. It was not the first of the month, so we all knew that we were going to the liquor store. We walked a little taller that day; I guess it was because of the Strawberry Festival. Clyde was in exceptionally good spirits and very much in charge of our trip. He was the only one who ever bought anything at the liquor store.

Once inside the store, with all the shiny, sparkling bottles lining the wall, Mitch began to shop. He would pick out the prettiest bottles and line them up on the counter as if he intended to buy them. As fast as he lined them up I would pick them up and put them back on the shelves. It was a game we played while Clyde did the real shopping. The clerk was used to Mitch's stubbornness and my persistence, so he watched us without comment. Mitch came over with two large bottles and placed them on the counter. I picked them up and put them back on the shelves. This went on until Mitch finally tired of the game, as he usually did, and we both went over to wait by the door while Clyde paid for three medium-sized bottles of sloe gin. It was a sweet, reddish-colored liquor that I had never tasted before. I assumed it to be a treat for the festival.

Although I never drank with Clyde and Mitch, they never offered me anything. I did drink with them this day, because when he had gotten back to the dealership, Clyde gave Mitch and me a bottle each. We sat with our backs to the wall and opened the small red jugs. There was a plastic seal around the lid, and I noticed that Mitch couldn't get his open. I walked over and tried to take the bottle from him to open it. Mitch clung to the bottle, and I had to use my fingernail to tear loose the plastic seal while he held onto it.

I had had four or five big drinks of the sloe gin

when I first began to sing. Adding a tune to one of the few rhymes that I knew, I sang:

> "Claudia Barnes, Claudia Barnes
> Has three husbands and a farm
> Raises hay and sells the hay
> Has three husbands by the way"

Clyde reached over and put his hand over the top of my bottle. Nodding toward Mitch, he said, "He'll learn that."

I knew what he meant. Mitch would put Claudia Barnes into his monologue, and it wouldn't do any of us any good.

I quit singing, got up and went out to the sidewalk and leaned against a utility pole. Every time a car would go by I would spit in the street where the passersby could see me. My mouth finally got dry, so I finished my sloe gin and swayed up Hill Avenue toward the trailer park.

Walking back to my own trailer, I felt a sense of euphoria. I took stock of my mind and body. My mind seemed to be working all right. I was thinking some happy thoughts. I was not afraid. My body seemed to be functioning well. I could see with my eyes, I could smell the fresh night air, I could feel the pavement under my feet, I could hear the noises of the traffic, and I felt at home and at peace in the world. It was the first time in my life that I marveled at my own being and ability. I leaped into the air, twisting my body completely around and landing on my feet again. I thought of a star so distant that no man had ever thought of a star as being so far away. I thought of a world so big and beautiful that only I knew the complete and complex meaning of it. I thought of myself as being much larger than the universe. I stood millions of miles tall and grasped a star in my palm and held it flat against the blackness of space and watched it twinkle and explode like a firecracker at Christmas. I picked up a small planet and looked for a deer running through tiny woods. I gently released the planet and watched it turn slowly in orbit. I looked about for God and realized that I must be He. And then I returned to my normal size, shaken and afraid.

 Dr. John Friend made a fool of himself at the reception given at Windfield Waycross' white colonial mansion. He urinated off the terrace of the place onto a couple who were dressed in evening clothes. It was not intentional. The young couple had walked around the side of the house to embrace one another and sneak a drink from a small flask. Dr. Friend, thinking he was safely in the dark, looked down a row of shrubs and bushes and urinated long and proudly off the terrace. He took his ability to "project" in such circumstances as a sign of good health.

There was a considerable row inside the house when Dr. Friend descended the stairs undetected and looking innocent. The young man, who had determined the nature of the liquid that had rained down upon them, was shouting, "I don't give a damn what you say, someone pissed off the porch on us!"

Mrs. Friend sat at the end of a long, gleaming table of flowers, food, and strawberries and cried. Her red-graying head was down on her short, fat arms and she sobbed so pitifully that the attention of the crowd in the hall was drawn away from the comedy of that scene to the contrasting attitude of Mrs. Friend. Several of the women in the house, including Mrs. Waycross, ran to Mrs. Friend and inquired about her anguish. The young couple was escorted outside, and the house was soon quiet except for the sobbing of Buffet Friend.

It was sad. John Friend would not have done such a thing deliberately. It was just that he had no eye and ear for such things. He collected no art, he paid little attention to music, he only cared for clothes that were particularly comfortable, and he was not famous for his smile. It frustrated Buffet Friend when she tried to instruct and interest him in such things. If there is a word for it, John Friend *plodded* through life. He stood in the hallway and rubbed his thumb on his pocket watch. He mentioned to one of the guests that the weather was perfect for the festival.

I was on my way up the street to the trailer, where the man who had rented it for the festival was cooking a steak for the fat lady who ran the milk bottle game at the carnival. I passed the laundromat and saw several people washing clothes. It dawned on me that they washed their clothes in these places all of the time. I walked to the window and looked in to see a woman in tight black britches and a shiny white top stuffing some very delicate pieces of clothing into one of the small washers. She had a cigarette dangling from her lips, and although her body seemed young and firm, her face was pale and her eyebrows had all but been removed. I walked in and sat down on one of the benches that lined the walls and picked up a farm magazine and started leafing through it. The carnival lady came over and sat down closer to me than I expected. There were a lot of people in the laundromat, and I thought that she could have found a more private seat. She spoke to me in an unfamiliar accent. "Wat time do da pebble heah blow off da lite?"

I was not sure I understood her, but I replied, "Ten, at the latest."

"Yoo da bick stayer-upper roun?"

"I stay up late."

"Snakes crawl in da nite."

"I'm in the marines. I got wounded in a practice fight, and they sent me home for a while. I just dropped in here because they're having the Strawberry Festival this week."

I think by now the lady thought I was drunk. She propped her arm on her crossed legs and puffed on her cigarette and said, "Da practice fitin in da marines now?"

"Yeah, we're using real bullets. Six guys got killed on a mountain the other day, and we couldn't carry them into camp, so we buried them right there and had some guy play a sad tune on the trumpet for them."

"Wat's dis boay doin on a mountain wid a trumpet?"

"He was on dope."

"Hmmnn."

"Well, look, I got to go see some friends and stuff—bye."

I got up and staggered, limping to the door, and heard her call after me, "Don shoot yeself in da foot, huh huh."

I made my way to a tree in the trailer park, either passed out or fell asleep, and dreamed that I fought some dreadful enemy far into the morning, when I awoke wet with dew and sick to my soul.

I walked down Hill Avenue on the other side of the street, away from Mitch and Clyde, and sat down on a small slope across from my father's house. He came out on the front porch after an hour or so, saw me and waved me over. I explained that I didn't want to wake him up. He took my head in his hands and looked into my face for a second. "Whew, this is a hangover if I'm any kind of a doctor at all," he said.

I murmured, "My head won't stop hurting."

"Come on in the office."

I sat on the table where he examined patients; I kept my eyes closed. My father rummaged around in his store of medicines and handed me a green and white pill and half a glass of water. He put his hands on his hips and watched me take the pill and said, "Hold on a minute."

He went into the main part of the house and came back with a can of beer in his hand. "Drink this."

I smelled the beer and almost vomited. He looked at the beer and said, "There are no known cures for hangovers except another drink. I don't recommend it as a general medical practice because it leads to other problems, but since you're a novice at this sort of thing I'd suggest you drink this, lie still for ten minutes and refrain from regurgitating."

I took the cold beer from his hand and drank all of it as a child would take bad medicine. The taste was bitter but the liquid was cold, and so I lay back and dared not move.

I must have fallen asleep for some time, because it was later in the morning when my mother was speaking to me. "James, what are you doing here? Are you all right? Has your father seen you?"

I jumped up quickly and said, "Yes, Mother, I'm fine and Father has seen me. I'm okay. I had a headache."

My mother patted me on the shoulder, straightened my nonexistent collar and said, "You must write me a letter and tell me all about this."

She closed the door to the main house, and I stepped down from the table to the floor, feeling good about being free of the pain, and decided that drinking was not for me.

I wondered about being a marine. How was that? Why? I hoped the carnival would leave town soon and that I would never see the lady in the tight britches and white top again. I would grow older and my appearance would change, and if she were to see me somewhere, she would not recognize me as the marine who had practiced fighting.

I went up to the dealership. Mitch and Clyde did not seem to be concerned about the previous night's adventure. Mitch was doing his Strawberry Festival monologue, and Clyde was sewing a button on his coat. I mumbled, "Good morning," and went to sleep.

Claudia Barnes came running through the tobacco patch, her red hair flying and her breath coming in short gasps, and her husband knew that he was in for his annual beating and tried to run. Claudia caught him just as he turned his back, and she reached around his head to slap him soundly in the mouth with her huge hand. It was a burning blow, and the small man fell to the ground and tried to cover himself as best he could. He was shocked and numb now. He knew that he was being hurt, but he could not, as yet, assess the damage. She beat him about the back and in the ribs. She kicked his legs—it was always the legs— and he made some kind of sound of anguish, but he wasn't sure what it was. The legs! The legs! The legs! She kicked them, bit them, pounded on them with her huge fists—and finally bit him on the thigh and drew a great flow of blood that she tasted and he could feel seeping through his trousers. And then she was gone and it was done, and there would be no more this year. The other two husbands of Claudia Barnes would see him this evening, and they would know that they were next, and they would be powerless to prevent it and wary for the next week until the ritual had caught up with them, too.

Claudia Barnes bathed every night. It was a huge bathtub that she had installed in her farmhouse. It was scented with the finest bath oils money could buy. It was a one-and-one-half-hour ritual, and she never failed to perform it. She would sit and luxuriate in the warm water, paying particular attention to her huge legs, which she massaged and exercised in the warm, soft, scented water. Claudia Barnes would retire to her bedroom and lie nude in the huge bed, waiting for any one of her husbands to come to her. There was no conversation and no foreplay. It was there for them to enjoy, and she never praised them if there were three a night or none at all. Masturbation was strictly forbidden, and she would know if any one of them had wasted his gift in that perversion. And so it was that Claudia Barnes assured herself of attention. She would sometimes go three or four nights without a visitor. She never complained, she never questioned—and she treated each of them as if they were her masters. She would not force them to work before daylight or after dark. They were not allowed to make any trips outside Woodmont Coves, and were not allowed to have money in any large amounts.

That night, while sleeping under a canvas, out of the dew, the truth came to me like some giant omnipotent metaphor. It swept across the land like a bright wave of light, sweeping away all art, writing, painting, speech, color, food, drink, sex, talent, and reason. Leaving the earth in a white statuesque scene of . . . of—not marble but a better, more subtle substance that made the earth and all things in it permanently pure and unchangeable. And Jesus could not find fault with it, but there was someone laughing quietly and respectfully in the good, quiet light of purity.

I went to the shed behind my father's house and picked up some clean clothes. I walked the way across the field to the paint factory and entered the smooth white building where the showers and steam baths were. I liked the paint factory showers. They had been built by the government to do a study of toxic poisoning of paint workers. It was an elaborate display of gleaming stainless steel fixtures and polished redwood benches and tables. I couldn't imagine the cost of the project, although I had heard various amounts of money mentioned. The people who worked at the paint factory never used the showers much. The most regular people there were high school athletes away from school for the summer and people like me who did not have such nice facilities at home. The cards were signed by paint company executives each month and mailed to the federal government as if everyone there took a shower after each working day. How the government could learn anything from this farce of research was not known, but the paint company officials did not discourage anyone from using the facility, and the abundance of huge white towels and free soap and shampoo were a gift to the community; and so it was continued year after year by some bureaucratic efficiency that kept the money coming.

I stood under a steaming spray of hot water for more than a half hour that morning. I used more than enough of the free fluffy towels to dry myself and then filled out one of the cards by the door to show that a paint employee had washed away the toxic effects of making paint.

As I was leaving the building I met Willie Alexander coming through the gate to the place. The uniformed guard looked sternly at Willie and his two companions and said, "Gentlemen, I only want one person in a stall in there. If there is any hanky-panky at all I'll have you barred from here. I've warned you before."

Willie was wearing a white cloth of some kind around his wrist. He snapped it like a small whip and pleaded with the officer, "Don't we have the same right to be here as anyone else? Isn't this government property? We have our rights."

The guard came out of his little building now and, staring quizzically at the cloth around Willie's wrist, he said, "You ain't got no rights here at all. This is a company facility monitored by the government and that's my speech and what I said and what the law says goes and that's all I know."

Willie and his companions sort of danced by me, and, flipping his wrist scarf at me, said, "If you had friends, James, you wouldn't have to shower alone."

They giggled as they entered the building, and I nodded to the guard as I left. The guard asked, as he usually did, "Did you fill out a card?"

I assured him that I had and felt the old weariness of coping engulf me five minutes after the governmental baptism.

I walked up Market Street, past the Waycross

Funeral Home, and turned left on Main Street to Givens' Hardware Store. I met several people on the way. Some of them waved and spoke. It seemed that the Strawberry Festival brought out an openness in people. I walked around the back of the store and sat down on the loading ramp and planned to sit there until the carnival opened in the late afternoon; then I would go there and try for the knife in the nickel-operated crane game.

Mr. Givens came out of the store and stood on the loading dock behind me and said, "James, how would you like to earn something today?"

I turned and looked at the big man. He was over six feet, had a short haircut and a square, firm face that gave him an all-around athletic look. Mr. Givens liked to hunt and fish. His was the store where you could buy hunting licenses, rifles and ammunition. I looked back at him and said, "I don't want anything."

I heard his voice behind me again. "Well, now, you haven't been around for a few days. I don't need any stock work. I need some of those big red fishing worms, and I could pay you cash this time."

I thought of the crane-operated game where the knife was. Not turning around, I said, "A coffee can full for three dollars."

Mr. Givens was silent for a minute. Then he said, "Okay, no dirt, all worms."

I jumped to the ground and waited while he brought out the coffee can and a small shiny mattock with a red handle. "Don't take the price tag off that," he said.

"I won't."

I walked around the corner, back down Market Street and went around behind Strong's Supermarket. There were scattered cardboard boxes lying wet and close to the ground, a favorite hiding place for worms, and I could lift the boxes and dig around just below the surface and find the fat red fishing bait. It was not as easy to dig a coffee can full of worms as I had remembered, but I had over half a can when I heard footsteps. I could hear the traffic on the road behind me, so I had not noticed that Joe Morgan had parked his old pickup truck a few yards away. I turned and saw him standing there and immediately thought of him killing his wife. He carried an old tackle box and a couple of fishing poles in his left hand; his right hand was down inside the pocket of his old brown coat. He said, "You diggin' worms in my worm-diggin' place."

I didn't say anything. I just stared at him. He said, "Been gettin' my worms here for a lot of years."

I stared at him. He said, "What am I sposed to do for worms?"

I stared.

He said, "Won't you give me 'em worms and git you some more?"

I hit his toe with the mattock as hard as I could and ran, slipping and sliding on the wet cardboard boxes. As I rounded the corner at Market Street I heard the explosion of the gun. I am certain that my heart stopped beating for a second. He had either shot his pistol at me or in the air to frighten me. My body was so interested in getting away that it leaned forward, ahead of my feet, and I went sprawling into the gravel at the side of the street. I regained my footing and ran to Givens' Hardware Store. I went in the store by the front entrance and was so out of breath I could not talk for a few minutes. I stood at the back of the store, near the paint section, until I had gotten my breath. I was sure that Joe Morgan would follow me here and shoot me. He did not.

I put the mattock and the worms on the counter—somehow I had managed not to spill them—and waited for Mr. Givens to pay me the three dollars. I watched over my shoulder for the form of Joe Morgan, but he never came. I went across the street to the courthouse and police station and sat in the rest room all afternoon. I vomited several times and shook so violently that I sometimes thought my heart would stop again.

 Joe Morgan had nailed an old slab of wood across the door of the bedroom where he had killed his wife. He had hung a calendar from Givens' Hardware Store on the slab and forgotten the room. His chair at the little kitchen table was set with the back to the door and faced the little road that led up to his place. It was silent at Joe Morgan's place. While great adventures and dramatic scenes were played out constantly in his mind, Joe Morgan sat and stared down the road, smoked cigarettes and drank moonshine. He was not aware of the silence. There was an almost constant Boom! Boom! Boom! sound in his mind. He had taken the sound to be the real thing, and he sometimes

delighted in the regularity of it. He would walk around his kitchen in time to the music, laughing and laughing.

Meanwhile, Claudia Barnes discovered that Joe Morgan had been cutting pulpwood from the top of one of the many hills on her place. Claudia roamed and inspected her place with care. There was not a corner of the farm that she did not see at least once a month, and it was a large and irregular piece of geography. With her red hair flying and her strong, round legs pounding, she marched across hill and valley as if she were expecting to find some encroachment upon her property and her beloved trees. On finding that one corner adjoining Joe Morgan's property had been raped of the small, firm trees, she stood silent and strong and welcomed the chance to defend what was hers. She never questioned or doubted that it was Joe Morgan who had committed the crime. It was his work and she knew it. She went straight back to her house, into her car, around the bend and up the hill to Joe Morgan's house. He was not at home. She found the door of the place open and could smell the smoke and the moonshine which was, for Joe Morgan, a regular fare. Going back to her car, she found a sheet of paper and a pencil with which she wrote the following message:

> Joe Morgan,
> If you ever set foot on my property again
> it will be the last move you will ever make.
> Claudia Barnes

Claudia Barnes's big mistake may have been that she hung the note on the nail over the calendar of the late Mrs. Morgan's bedroom door. It was a small thing, and yet it was partly the position of the note that infuriated Joe Morgan. He did not see it immediately, and he wondered how long it had been there and if he had cut any wood since the note came. He didn't remove the note from the nail. He would stand and inspect it carefully from time to time as if he expected it to take on new meaning. Did she intend to shoot him? Of course not. She had never, to his recollection, fired a gun on her property. She intended to run him down and strangle him. He was sure of it. She could easily do it, too.

Joe Morgan took down his .30-06 rifle and looked through the scope at a white spot on a tree about 125 yards away. He put the rifle down and realized that it would have to be a much longer shot than that. Deciding that this project was too much of a shot to be mistaken, Joe Morgan decided to do some research. He got into his old pickup truck, placed his worn and shiny .38 special pistol on the seat beside him and drove to Friedman's Pharmacy. There was, he remembered, a large color poster showing all of the vital organs of the human body hanging on the hallway wall that led to the bathroom in the pharmacy. He parked his truck and tucked the gun into his belt and looked up and down the street before walking into the pharmacy to use the bathroom. The light in the hallway was dim, so he asked the young man at the front desk if there was a light switch in the hall. The young man explained that it was behind the door. Joe Morgan was standing looking at the huge color poster when Maude Primm came down the hallway toward the bathroom. "Oh, excuse me," she said.

"Ats okay. I'm not usin' the bathroom—let me ask you somethin', is everybody's heart located rite there?"

Maude Primm looked at the large poster and said, "Certainly."

"Thank ye."

Maude stood for a minute and watched as Joe Morgan walked down the hallway out into the pharmacy. She looked at the poster again and decided Joe Morgan had been having chest pains. She had put the poster there in order to readily answer the many questions people would ask about where a certain organ or function was situated in the human body. The appendix and the kidney were particularly smudged with fingerprints.

Dodd Givens looked up from the counter of his hardware store and said, "What can I do for you, Joe?"

Joe Morgan said, "I wonder if I'd hafta buy a whole box of them .30-06 shells if I just needed one or two?"

"They don't come loose, Joe. You have to buy a box. You must be planning on some fancy shooting if you just need two."

"How much is the box?"

"What grain bullet you want?"

"Uh, 180."

"I can let you have them special for eight dollars and forty cents."

Joe Morgan reached into his pocket and came out with some very old and worn dollar bills.

"You see anybody wants to buy some loose, you let me know," he said.

Claudia Barnes stood on her back porch by the washing maching and heard the rifle shots. They were distant and came in groups of threes. She walked to the window of the enclosed porch and stared off in the direction of the shots. They seemed to be out of place in the warm weather. It was generally a shotgun or a pistol shot from the Morgan side of the country that was heard in the summer. The louder, sharp sound of the rifle was heard mostly in the winter, when the deer season was on. She shrugged her shoulders and went about her business when the shooting stopped. Little did she suspect that Joe Morgan was rehearsing her murder.

Joe Morgan walked to the tree where he had tacked the white piece of paper and noted that there were three bullet holes, one almost on top of the other. He wet his finger and tested the wind to make sure he would not need to adjust for windage when the all-important shot was made. It would have to be a clear day, and he would want Claudia Barnes to be between 250 and 350 yards away.

He went to his deer stand and looked up into the tree to see if it was intact. He laid his rifle on the ground and climbed to his seat some twenty-five feet in the tree. Taking his knife from his pocket, he trimmed away a branch that had grown across his line of sight. And he waited.

It was not until five days later that his target came into view. Joe Morgan had come to his stand every day from daylight until noon and waited for Claudia Barnes to make one of her inspection trips. He had carelessly strewn an array of whiskey bottles, sausage cans, and cracker wrappers around the bottom of the tree during his vigil.

Claudia Barnes walked swiftly and proudly to where she knew Joe Morgan cut down her trees. It was to this destination he thought she would return. She had decided she would find him and beat him if more trees were missing.

Joe Morgan laid his rifle across the strong limb in front of him and leveled the scope to where he could see the huge figure of Claudia Barnes marching. He whistled softly into the quiet morning air. Claudia Barnes stopped. She looked around as if she were not sure she had heard anything at all. Joe Morgan whistled again. She turned in his direction and stepped upon a rock to get a better view into the dark-green, leafy forest. Joe Morgan took a deep breath, let half of it out, centered the scope on the heart of his prey and squeezed the trigger.

There were four people in the truck when it pulled up in front of the courthouse and police station of Woodmont Coves. Three husbands sat cramped in the front, and the dead body of Claudia Barnes lay uncovered in the back. The smallest man went into the police station and announced to Jimmy Barrett, the chief of police, that Joe Morgan had shot Claudia Barnes with a deer rifle.

Including Jimmy Barrett, there were almost a hundred people standing staring at the body of Claudia

Barnes when the ambulance from the Waycross Funeral Home arrived. The body was taken away, and the state police and Jimmy Barrett went out to Joe Morgan's house to charge him with murder.

At the trial Maude Primm said that Joe Morgan had been looking for the exact location of the human heart; Dodd Givens said Joe Morgan had bought shells from him; the state police found the junk Joe Morgan had left around the tree, and a lady said he had bought such items from her store. It went on and on, and Joe Morgan was convicted and committed as criminally insane.

The defense wanted to know why each of the husbands had been beaten recently, but no answer was forthcoming.

> Claudia Barnes, Claudia Barnes
> Had three husbands and a farm
> Raised the hay and sold the hay
> Morgan shot her by the way

I did not get the four-bladed, dark-brown wooden-handled knife from the crane game at the carnival. I tried. I spent four dollars watching the small toy crane dig into the pile of assorted trinkets. The crane was maneuverable, but each time the knife was almost within reach, it would slip from the bucket and crash back into the pile, leaving me with a toy whistle or nothing at all. At the time I did not consider that the knife might be too heavy for the small crane—as many of the other, better, choices might have been.

I walked around the carnival grounds and looked at the many stakes that had been driven into the ground to hold the tents that housed almost every attraction. I had watched on several occasions as the men drove the huge metal stakes into the ground and had admired the rhythm and boring regularity with which they swung the huge, heavy hammers. The arduous task of driving the stakes was partially relieved by the singsong grunts of the workers, and occasionally a song of sorts would break out among the crew. Oomph-hah, Oomph-hah, Oomph-hah. They were lean, tattooed men who swung the hammers; I thought someone had given them a collective name, but I could not remember what it was.

Several of the barkers at the carnival called me by name and inquired as to how my father, the doctor, was doing. I saw the fat lady at her milk bottle stand and I saw the girl in the black britches and white top cooking hamburgers and french fries—but I avoided that row of tents and watched a wretched person invite people into a tent to see an even more wretched person eat a live chicken and drink its blood. I watched the Ferris wheel turn lazily against the summer evening sky and heard the screams of the people on the tilt-a-whirl. Music was everywhere, and it ran into itself on many occasions and caused a mild uproar of melody and rhythm that could not be comprehended or appreciated. I thought about joining the carnival and running away on some great adventure until it dawned on me that I was afraid of these world-wise people and their mysterious pasts. I was also mildly surprised to think that Woodmont Coves was more than enough of a puzzle, and that adventure was not as far distant as I might have once imagined it to be.

There was no more participating that I wanted to

do at the carnival, and yet I could not leave it. I climbed a small hill above the grounds on which the carnival surged and subsided and watched the flow of rural folk and townspeople mill about in the huge watercolored summer evening.

I watched the scene for over an hour before walking back down Hill Avenue to Second Street and to the liquor store, where I bought a small bottle of sloe gin. My hangover forgotten, I desperately wanted to be God again.

I sipped the sloe gin. The feeling was warm, and I replayed my heroics with Joe Morgan of a few days ago. It was an act of bravery, I thought. In replaying the scene for my entertainment, I took the gun away from him and marched him into Jimmy Barrett's office and demanded that he be locked up as a menace to the community. I slapped him about the face and made him admit that he had killed his wife. I was rewarded with a huge sum of money from some obscure league of justice. It was with this attitude of confidence that I hid my bottle of sloe gin behind a garbage can and walked into the Main Street Diner. Maude Primm sat at the back of the diner looking firm and smooth in a black cocktail dress. I walked as steadily as I could to the back of the diner and sat down at a booth opposite and across the way from Maude.

I ordered a hamburger with everything and stirred my fingers in the ice water, wishing that I had another drink of sloe gin. Maude looked over at me and said, "Hi, James, I'm really sorry you don't love me anymore." She laughed a small laugh.

I said, "A marine is a marine is a marine."

She said, "What's that about? Have you joined the marines?"

"Oh, nothing, I guess."

"Have you joined the marines?"

"Not yet."

"You should come by and see me. I have to run an errand, but you could wait in the apartment for me. I'll only be a few minutes."

"Bring me a bottle of sloe gin."

"Oh, is the big marine drinking now?"

"I'll be there; you just bring it."

I turned my face to the wall of the diner and pretended to examine the light fixture over the booth. I heard the rustle of clothes as Maude Primm left the booth, and I turned my attention to the hamburger and Coke the waitress had brought. The waitress said, "We close in ten minutes."

I said, "Okay."

I was just finishing the hamburger when Maude Primm came back into the diner and pressed something into my hand. "The keys," she said.

"Oh, yeah."

"See you in a few minutes."

"All right."

I went outside to the garbage can and retrieved my bottle and walked to Maude Primm's apartment. I finally found the key for the lock on the key ring and let myself into the small apartment. I found the light switch and turned on a bright overhead light. A huge bulb shone overhead, so I switched on the blue light over the bed and turned out the overhead light. I sat down on one of the chairs and took a long drink from my bottle. I looked around the small apartment and noticed that the large white freezer Maude kept her medicine in was now locked with a huge brass padlock. I knew that there used to be some medicine stored in the freezer, but it had never been locked before. I shook out the keys on the ring she had given me and noticed a new brass key among the rest. I walked over to the freezer and tried it in the lock and found that it worked. I removed the lock and lifted the lid and looked into the frozen face of Dr. Friedman.

I must have screamed or made some kind of noise because I was sitting on the floor when I realized what I had seen. I slowly got to my feet and took another look. And there, in a sitting position with his funeral suit on, his arms at his sides, his legs stretched along the bottom of the freezer, was the late Dr. Friedman, looking almost alive. It had to be the makeup, but he looked perfectly preserved except for a small dot of frost at the corner of his lips. I touched him to make sure it was him and not the effects of the sloe gin. He was hard and stony. I closed the lid and turned on the overhead light.

I went and sat down at the edge of the bed. I tried to think. I didn't know what kind of thinking was required. There must be a special kind of thinking one must do on such occasions. I decided to think small. "There is a body in the freezer . . . it is the body of someone you know . . . do something."

I looked back to the freezer. I tried high thinking.

"God makes such things possible . . . there are universal needs and wants . . . you must not consider this to any great extent . . . be calm."

I became calm, or so I thought.

I heard Maude Primm coming up the stairs and waited as she opened the door. She immediately saw the keys and lock lying on the floor and knew that I had opened the freezer. She came to me at the side of the bed and said, "James, I can explain this."

I said nothing.

She said, "I don't want to talk about it now. Would you like to have some chicken noodle soup?"

I must have agreed to have some soup, because soon I was sitting and eating the soup from a white bowl with blue flowers printed on it. I liked Maude Primm's chicken noodle soup. It reminded me of the good cans of chicken and dumplings Mitch and Clyde often had on special days. I slowly ate the soup and listened to Maude saying, "Dr. Friedman believed in cryonics. He wanted his body frozen so that if a cure were found for his disease, the cause of his death, he could be restored to good health and continue to live. Do you understand?"

I shook my head yes. I looked at Maude Primm and started to ask how there could be a cure for murder. I got as far as "how" and then went back to eating the soup.

I finished the soup and went for the bottle of sloe gin she had brought back with her. I took two long, slow drinks and went to lie down on the bed.

Maude came to me and pulled off my shoes and

socks; she proceeded to undress me and make comforting little statements about me being a marine and a good boy and such things, until she was in bed with me and we were making love. It must have been the shock of seeing Dr. Friedman in the freezer, or the sloe gin, but we made better bed partners that night than we had ever been before.

I awoke the next morning with my father's advice on my mind. The only cure, he had said, for a hangover was another drink; so I lifted the small bottle of sloe gin from the floor and drained it before lying back down to wait for the pain in my head to stop. I found myself having sex with Maude again in the early morning light. She rolled toward me and put one of her legs across mine, and I took it as a cue and obliged her.

I was almost down the stairs when I remembered all that had happened the night before. I walked back up the stairs, into the room and over to the freezer, and Dr. Friedman was still there, still cold, and I thought, still dead.

I walked down Hill Avenue in the early-morning sunshine and was aware that I didn't want anything. I didn't want food, sex, money, sleep, rain, sun—nothing. I didn't want anything. It was a strange feeling to not care what was coming, what would happen or where I was going. I stopped and found a seat against the wall with Mitch and Clyde.

I was sitting listening to Mitch's latest monologue and wondering about the origin of it. "Now, you take breathing, comes easy and roughlike at times, hear that? I tol you once and two, three time that it ain't cool to breath so nice and have stopping and stuff in there. Got it? Roll on down and hear yourself breathe if you've a mind to; but don't pay no 'tention to air cause it might not and then again it might come a lot; so there ain't no use in worrying it . . . okay? Hmmnn? That so, you know that?"

I turned to Clyde, who was awake and cleaning his fingernails with a knife, and said, "It worries me."

Clyde said, "I know."

I wanted desperately to talk to someone, and I knew of no one I could talk with. I could write my mother a letter, but my typewriter was in the trailer and she couldn't, or didn't want to, read my handwriting. I sat against a tree and composed a letter in my mind.

Dear Mother,

I know you won't believe this, but Maude Primm has Dr. Friedman in her freezer and intends to keep him there. Mitch and Clyde are the best friends I have, and they are winos. I am a grown man and I don't know anything. I am not interested in knowing anything. I feel sorry for you. I am not proud of my father. He lives so simply and so stupidly. While he has dismissed me as "curious," I would like you to know that I believe I have inherited my trait from him. I told a total stranger that I was wounded in the marines. I have been having sex with Maude Primm. There! Aren't you surprised at some of the things I know? Some of the things I do?

This letter will never be mailed. And now that I've written it, I wonder what it is that you know and that I don't know.

Give my regards all around, and tell people you

have talked with me and that I am fine. Congratulations on your table decorations at the Strawberry Festival reception.

    Your loving son,

    James

I walked on down the bank of the Boo River until I came to the rear of Strong's Supermarket. I went around front to the beer cooler and bought a six-pack of cold beer. The clerk put it in a brown paper bag, and I walked up the street to the dealership and again found a seat against the warm wall with Mitch and Clyde.

I was as thirsty as I have ever been. I drank three of the beers and began to feel comfortable and alive again. I started to sing:

"From this valley they say you are going . . ."

Mitch stopped his monologue and looked at me for a minute. I continued to sing and to smile. Mitch rolled over on his stomach and got to his feet by way of his hands and knees and started a little dance. We were having a good old time for a few minutes until I saw Mitch suddenly sit down against the wall with a frown on his face. I looked around and saw Jimmy Barrett sitting in his police car parked alongside the curb. He rolled down the window on the passenger's side and said in a loud voice, "Some of this stuff amounts to disturbing the peace. You boys better hold it down."

I said "Yes, sir" loud enough for him to hear me and he drove off. I looked at Clyde, who had been patting his foot to the music, and he just shrugged his shoulders. Mitch began a monologue on the police. It started to rain and Mitch and Clyde went to their shed. I walked and ran around to the loading ramp at Givens' Hardware Store and finished my beer.

 Windfield Waycross of the Waycross Funeral Home came to take the lobsterlike body of Dr. Friedman from the apartment on the morning that it was discovered by Jimmy Barrett. Maude had gone down to the funeral home to make the arrangements. She swallowed several white pills on the way to the funeral home and made no pretense about her grief—or lack of it. Windfield came out of the back room of the funeral home with his best look of condolence; Maude Primm took out a note pad and said, "Windfield, I have a few questions to ask you."

"Of course, my dear, and what would it be first?"

"Well, don't call me 'dear.' I've known you for a number of years, and it bothers me. Call me Maude."

"Very well."

"Now this is a question that I'm not sure you can answer, but I have to know something about it."

"Fire away."

"What is cryonics, anyway?"

"My goodness, why do you ask a question like that? We don't have any service like that here."

"I didn't think so." Maude looked out the window for a moment and then said, "What would a thing like that cost?"

Windfield Waycross flipped through a little book he held in his hand as if he expected to find a figure. "Well, I couldn't say. It's a newfangled idea of some kind, but I certainly can't recommend it."

"It was a last wish of the doctor."

"Really?"

"Yes."

"Well, I'll be."

"Strange request, don't you think?"

"We've taken some people to Middletown to have them cremated, but I never ever participate in that; we just bring home the ashes."

"What are you doing to the doctor now?"

"They are embalming him. It's the customary practice and, in fact, it is required by law."

Maude Primm sat down on a chair and rubbed her hands together for a moment. Then she said, "I don't think this cryonics thing involves embalming, does it?"

"I don't believe so, but I believe these things have to be worked out by a person while he is living. Are you sure this was his final wish?"

"I'm sure of it, although it is not a part of his will."

"There, well now, he was an old man and could have been given to some sort of wishful thinking about living forever, or some such thing. I don't believe I'd take his idea too seriously."

Maude looked out the window again and got up from the chair. "What time will the body be ready for viewing?" she asked.

"Well, no later than three this afternoon."

Maude closed her notebook and said, "Blue suit, red tie, white shirt, black shoes. I want a brown economy casket, concrete vault, and I want the service conducted by Reverend Turner. The funeral will be tomorrow at three."

Windfield Waycross was writing as fast as he could, but he looked up abruptly and said, "So soon?"

"Tomorrow at three."

"As you wish. Red tie?"

"Red tie."

Maude made a note in her little book and said to Windfield Waycross, "Don't mention this cryonics business to anyone else, if you don't mind."

"Not at all, not at all."

Windfield Waycross watched the long figure of Maude Primm marching up the street. Then he turned to get to his desk and find that pamphlet on this business of freezing people to be cured and brought back to life in future years. As if he were looking for the name in a phone book, he repeated, "Cryonics, cryonics?"

Maude Primm went back to the little apartment where Dr. Friedman had lived. She sat down on the bed for a minute and held her head in her hands. She got up and paced the floor for a few minutes. Her eyes caught the freezer, standing white and out of place in the small room. She went to it and lifted the lid, knowing what she would see but examining the amount of room in it. It was a large chest-type freezer, and there were only a few packages of medicine on one side of it. She took the boxes of drugs from the freezer and crawled into it. She attempted to sit down and realized that if she were a little smaller she would be able to manage it.

She took the boxes of medicine and walked hurriedly to Strong's Supermarket. She saw Lydia Strong, wife of Bo Strong, the owner, stacking groceries in the rear of the store. She walked toward her with the boxes of medicine and asked, "Lydia, how are you?"

Lydia Strong dusted her hands together and said, "Oh, Maude, I'm so sorry to hear about Dr. Friedman. It was awful."

"It was an awful shock to everybody. Lydia, would you mind storing these things in your freezer for me for a few days?"

"Why, we'd be happy to do anything we can for you, Maude. When will the services be held?"

"Tomorrow at three o'clock."

"So soon?"

"Last wish."

"Oh, I see. I was planning to have my hair done."

"I have to run, Lydia. Thank you so much. We'll see you tomorrow."

Maude Primm stopped at her house for a moment and then got into her car. She had brought a bed sheet with her, and she folded it neatly on the front seat and drove to the rear of the Waycross Funeral Home. Windfield Waycross was combing the mustache of Dr. Friedman when she walked in.

Windfield turned and said proudly, "Doesn't he look natural?"

Maude came slowly toward the casket and looked into the face of her departed employer. "He looks okay," she said.

Maude Primm sat down on the small metal chair in

the preparation room and looked around. She was looking for something in particular—the key wrench that would close a casket and lock it. She got up and walked around the room and saw a set of keys, obviously the keys to the funeral home, hanging on a well-worn peg behind the door; on that ring was the key she wanted. She walked back over to where Windfield Waycross was fussing over his customer. "Windfield, could you do me a favor, could you find me a cigarette?"

He looked up from his work and said, "I didn't know you smoked."

"I usually don't, but with so much pressure I . . ."

"Oh, yes, well, that happens a lot here. Let me see if I can find you one somewhere." He went off into another part of the building.

Maude Primm grabbed the phone and dialed Strong's Supermarket. Lydia Strong answered. Maude said, "Lydia, call me back at the funeral home right away, will you please?" and she hung up.

Windfield Waycross returned and handed her a pack of stale cigarettes. "It's all I could find. Someone must have left them here."

Maude stayed very close to the phone and looked around for a match. Windfield Waycross became aware that she didn't have a match just as the phone rang. Maude grabbed the phone and said, in a startled voice, "Where? When? Yes! Yes!" She put the phone back on the hook and said, "There's been a terrible accident on Route Fifty-two West. They want an ambulance!"

Windfield whirled in a frenzy. He grabbed two

blankets off a nearby chair and ran for the door. He turned to Maude and said, "I'll be right back . . . right back, uh, you okay?"

Maude Primm opened the door for him and said, "I'll be fine. You do what you have to do."

Windfield Waycross did not want to miss an opportunity like this. It was the rule in the funeral home business that whoever got a blanket over a body first was entitled to handle the funeral services. There could be as many as six or seven people in a real bad accident. He hoped there were no children; he hated doing children. He could never satisfy anyone with a child. They never looked natural. Old people didn't look natural either, for that matter, but you could improve on old age. He was thinking these thoughts as his sleek new Cadillac ambulance roared down Market Street and out to Route 52.

Back at the funeral home Maude Primm answered the phone again. It was Lydia Strong. "What in the world is going on over there, Maude? You hung up on me."

"Oh, nothing, Lydia. Windfield has been called out on an ambulance run, and the phones are messed up. I just called you to tell you that I checked, and the service is at three tomorrow."

"Oh, thank you. Are you sure you're all right?"

"I'm just fine, Lydia, thank you. Bye."

Hanging up the phone, Maude Primm went down the small set of steps and out the back door of the funeral home. She grabbed the bed sheet from the front of the car and ran back inside. She took another short look at the small body in the casket and then picked it out of the brown economy resting place and wrapped the sheet around it. She walked rather slowly down the steps this time, as she had not realized the body would be so heavy. She placed the draped body on the floor of the back seat of the car. Running back inside, she carried two concrete blocks from the trunk of her car that were beginning to feel much heavier than the body had been. She put one of the blocks at each end of the casket and slammed the lid. She breathed a sigh of relief and then picked the key wrench off the hook and began to screw in the bolts that locked the casket. When she had secured the bolts, she sat back and wiped the perspiration from her brow.

The phone rang. She picked it up and said hello in a calm but breathless voice. It was Windfield Waycross.

"Maude, is that you?"

"Yes."

"Have you heard anything from Jimmy Barrett? There ain't no accident out here on Fifty-two."

Windfield Waycross was gone far longer than Maude Primm had expected. He had driven around checking other possible places for accidents; once she heard him go screaming past the bus station at the other end of First Street on Hill Avenue. He came into the funeral home carrying the extra blankets he had taken and asked, "Have you heard anything? Who closed the casket?"

"I haven't heard anything. I closed the casket. It must have been a crank call."

"You closed the casket? You can't do that."

"It's done. It will be a closed funeral."

"In a red tie?"

"It's closed."

Windfield Waycross sat down on a chair, a little sus-picious. He looked around the room and said, "I'll have to double-check everything and lock it."

"It's locked."

"It's locked?" Windfield got up and went to the cas-ket and looked at the secure bolts in place and said, "You did that?"

Maude stood defiant now. "Yes, I locked it, and it remains locked because there's jewelry and some other things in there that the doctor wanted in there, and I'll not have them pilfered!"

Windfield held out his arms in defeat and said, "Maude, if this is the way you want this thing done, we'll do it this way, but I swear you are the most darndest person I have ever dealt with. What makes you think anyone would steal from the dead?"

"Thank you, Windfield."

Windfield Waycross had built up a very nice little business stealing from the dead. He had a man who came by every three months for some very nice pieces of jewelry and wedding rings that people had foolishly tried to bury forever. Windfield thought it was stupid to bury things of value. It was not stealing from the dead, either. When someone died, they left whatever they owned to their heirs, and if they were stupid enough to bury it, then you were stealing from the stupid living and not the stupid dead. That was Windfield's philosophy, and he intended to steal that jewelry—and God knows how many other valuables—from the casket tomorrow.

Maude Primm spent the night at the funeral home. She took two small pills with her coffee and refused to leave the room where the casket was except to go to the bathroom. Although she was bright-eyed, she had a disheveled look by late morning when people started arriving to pay their respects. There were some questions about why the body could not be viewed, but they were answered in whispers of "final wish."

Maude's all-night vigil and rumpled appearance gave her the look of a bereaved person.

The body of Dr. Friedman lay in the back seat of Maude's car, located in the parking lot at the rear of the funeral home. The car was not locked.

Three o'clock approached, and the townspeople gathered and sat in the wooden folding chairs in front of the casket. Reverend Bill Turner stood with head bowed, as if he were in some silent prayer. Windfield Waycross quietly closed the doors of the small chapel to keep the street traffic noise down and stood at the back of the room keeping watch as one of his employees drove the hearse to the front of the building. Reverend Turner cleared his throat as a signal that the service was about to begin. He turned the pages of his Bible and said, "We are not gathered here today to bury Dr. Friedman."

Maude Primm's head snapped up quickly, drawing the attention of several mourners. Reverend Turner continued, "We are here today to bury the worldly temple of a righteous and beloved brother in Christ . . ."

Windfield Waycross stepped outside the chapel door and slipped silently outside to make sure everything was in readiness at the cemetery. He was assured that all was well.

The service ended and the pallbearers walked slowly out the door with the casket. Maude Primm walked out the back door and got into her car. She glanced into the backseat to see if her passenger was still there. He was, and she drove around to the front of the funeral home and parked behind the hearse.

As the funeral procession moved slowly down Route 52, Windfield crawled over the backseat of the hearse into the darkened interior of the rear. Taking his key wrench from his pocket, he quickly unlocked the casket and raised the lid. Removing the small penlight from his pocket, he shone it down on the white interior of the casket and two concrete blocks. He was in shock for a second or two. He sat on the floor of the hearse holding the light and staring at the two concrete blocks lying flat and dirty against the satin lining of the casket. He reached his hand inside to feel one of the blocks to assure himself that they were real. He could not determine how long he sat there, and it dawned on him that they might be approaching the grave site. He closed the lid, locked the casket and crawled back into the front seat. He was perspiring and shaking as he settled back into his seat in the front of the hearse. The driver asked, "Everything okay?"

Windfield Waycross nodded his head that everything was. He was certain he had been trapped for stealing jewelry from his customers. He looked suspiciously at the driver and said, "Did you see any people that we don't know at the shop this morning?"

"I don't believe so."

"I mean, anybody who looked like he might be nosing around or anything?"

"Everybody looked kind of ordinary to me. Is something wrong?"

"I don't think so, but these damned federal and state officials are nosing around in a guy's business, and it just pisses me off, that's all. I want to get this service over with and take a day or two off; this business is wearing me out."

"I thought you liked this business?"

"I do, but it's not like it used to be. People don't have the reverence for funerals that they used to have, or something. I don't know."

It dawned on Windfield Waycross that Maude Primm had stolen the body of Dr. Friedman. What did she do with it? What the hell did she want with it? Well, one thing was dead certain: He was not going to raise any hell about it. He was going to bury those concrete blocks, collect his money, and not know any more than he was supposed to know. It would not be the first time, for that matter, that a director buried bricks, sand or concrete blocks. People were strange about death, and human bodies were valuable even after they were dead. He knew that.

After the service was over and Maude Primm returned to her car, Lydia Strong came running over and said, "Maude, could you drive me back by the market? Bo is going to come back with the pallbearers."

"Sure. Hop in. Oh, has it ever been a long day."

"It sure has. I couldn't get my hair fixed, and it's a mess. Say, what do you have there in the backseat?"

Maude Primm tensed for a second and then said, "Oh, that's something that belonged to Dr. Friedman."

I don't suppose any of the following would have happened had I not gone to the bus station to find something to read. It was now the fourth day of the Strawberry Festival, and Mitch had been on one of his crying routines. It still depressed me to see such sadness and to be so helpless about it.

I looked around the bus station for a paperback, but there were none. I settled for a newspaper from Middletown that someone had dropped off on the way through town. I folded it under my arm and walked back up Hill Avenue on the opposite side of the street from Mitch and Clyde. They were sitting against the wall, and I could see that Mitch had gotten over his spell of crying and was trying to get the circulation back into his right leg—a project he pursued from time to time.

I walked over to where they were and sat down in my customary place, unfolded the newspaper, and started looking through it. The following ad caught my eye at once:

THE LAUGHING MAN
(ONE SHOW ONLY)
EAST PARKER HIGH SCHOOL GYM
7:30 P.M. TONITE

I checked the date of the paper and discovered it

was current and that the show would take place tonight. I turned to Clyde, who was rubbing his hands together, and said, "The Laughing Man is putting on a show in Middletown tonight."

Mitch kept rubbing his hands and said, "Twenty-six miles, too far."

I got up and walked out to the street and looked at the traffic. It wasn't much at ten in the morning. I wanted to get out of town, I wanted to see The Laughing Man, and I had the money, so I started walking up Hill Avenue to Hill Road, where I knew the traffic would be headed toward Middletown. It took me about fifteen minutes to make the walk, and I was a little out of breath when I reached the intersection where River Road and Hill Road met. I walked out to the wide place between the two roads and sat down for a minute. An old pulpwood skeeterbug came rambling down the River Road, turned into the wide place and came to a halt. A small, dark young man with a black beard walked to the edge of the bushes and tossed a beer can into the weeds as he urinated onto the ground. I walked to where the skeeterbug was parked and stood nearby until he came back. As he was coming toward me I asked, "You going to Middletown?"

"Hop right in."

I got into the front seat of the convertible rig and was glad that it was not one of those skeeterbugs with wood loaded all around. I would have not wanted to ride to Middletown on a pile of pulpwood. The small young man at the wheel reached behind his seat and took out a can of beer. "Want one?" he asked.

"Believe I will."

He reached his hand out and said, "I'm Mose Random. Ain't you Doc Friend's son?" I shook his hand and told him that I was.

It was good to be getting out of Woodmont Coves. It was good to have a cold beer in my hand. The past few days had made me somehow aware of my entire past in my hometown. As the old skeeterbug rambled down toward the bridge across the Boo River, I could feel the weight of Dr. Friedman's body, Maude Primm's body, and the laundromat girl's body slide off my shoulders.

Mose Random spoke loudly over the noise of the skeeterbug. "You got some business in Middletown?"

"The Laughing Man is over there tonight."

"He is?"

"Yep."

"Hey, maybe I'll go with you if you don't mind. That guy is fun to watch."

"I'd be glad to have some company."

"My friends call me Mosey. You can call me Mosey if you want to. What's your name?"

"James. Nobody calls me Jim, just James."

"If your name's James, they oughta call you James."

"Jim is short for James. A lot of people called James are called Jim," I said, thinking how stupid it sounded.

The short, dark boy named Mosey said, "Why'd they want to do that?"

"I don't know."

I took a long drink of the beer to change the subject.

We rode quietly along the smooth stretch of road across the bottomland on the other side of the river.

I was startled to hear Mosey say, "What about the marines?"

I looked at him suspiciously. "What about the marines?"

"You just said, 'To hell with the marines.'"

"I just said, 'to hell with the marines?'"

"Yep."

"I didn't say anything about the marines."

"You sure did. You were sitting there looking down the road and said, 'To hell with the marines.'"

I realized that I was probably thinking out loud and said, "I'm sorry. I must have been thinking out loud."

"Were you in the marines?"

"Yeah." I lied again.

Mosey Random looked at me with a frown and said, "You want another beer?"

I snapped back from the scene in the laundromat and said, "I sure do, thank you."

We rode in silence for a few minutes, and then Mosey started singing:

> "Boys, don't go drinking and gambling,
> It'll drag you all down into hell
> Boys, don't go drinking and gambling,
> It'll drag you all down into hell"

Mosey finished the song in a low, mournful monotone, looked at me, gave a jerky nod of the head, and smiled to show a row of very white teeth. I smiled back at him and made the same jerky motion of the head, and we rolled on into Middletown, drinking one beer after another.

The Laughing Man was walking through a field behind his home in the country. He carried a shiny bottle in his hand, and he was crying. Sweat ran down his face as he pushed himself past his endurance in the foot-high grass. He stopped his march and threw the shiny bottle down on a flat rock. The bottle burst, and the sweet, addictive smell of scotch whiskey reached his nostrils as he fell to his knees. The Laughing Man was not laughing today. He looked toward the sky and shouted, "Are you out there? Is anybody out there?" Silence surrounded him as he waited for an answer. A defiant look came over his face as he stared at the heavens. He was waiting for, and expecting, lightning, thunder or death. There was a peaceful breeze across the meadow now. The Laughing Man noticed it immediately. He felt the cool breeze, and he was sure it was God in the air—and then he was not sure. He raised his voice to the heavens again. "Oh, no, no, no, no, no! That won't do. That's not enough. I've seen floods, fires, wars, hail, sleet, snow, oh, oh, I've seen it all, and you say God is just a gentle breeze." He began to laugh. A wild, crazy, crying kind of laugh. He stood and turned his body in circles like a small child playing. Twisting and laughing and crying, he suddenly became quiet. He stood with his body in a half twist. He straightened himself and listened for something—he didn't know what. He looked as if someone were about to speak. No one did. He began to laugh again. It was a loud, proud laugh, and he thought the joke was on him. It was a laugh of relief. It was not his professional laugh.

The breeze subsided.

Mosey Random and I rode the old skeeterbug into the scales at the Middletown Paper Mill. The odor was terrible around the place. It smelled as if someone had been suffering with a chronic case of flatulence, as my father would say. The man in the little shack beside the scales came out and said, "Two passengers."

Then he began to pound on the end of the pulp-wood with a hammer. I turned to Mosey and said, "What's he doing?"

"Looking for waterlogs. You can soak this wood in the creek for two weeks and it'll sell double."

"No water," the man shouted, as if he were talking to himself. Mosey and I threw the lengths of wood onto a conveyor belt and watched it ramble off into a huge wooden building to some unknown fate. We returned to the scales and parked the skeeterbug on them again. The man in the little shack shouted to himself again, "No water, two passengers."

He cranked a small pale-blue check out of a machine and handed it to Mosey. "Thank you, sir," Mosey said.

"No water, two passengers," the man said in a tone of finality.

Mosey parked the old skeeterbug in a line with several other old, similar vehicles and we walked across the parking area and up a steep street to a small café. There were several people there from the outskirts of Woodmont Coves who had brought their pulpwood to

Middletown. We sat on a pair of stools and ordered a beer and a hamburger each. Mosey took the check from his pocket and, borrowing a pencil from the waitress, signed the back of the check. "This twelve dollars and forty cents is our spending money," he said.

The waitress took the check and put it under the change drawer in the cash register and came back to the counter with the money. She counted it out to Mosey: ". . . nine, ten, eleven dollars and forty cents."

I said, "I thought it was twelve dollars and something."

Mosey said, "They always charge you a dollar to cash the check."

"Why?"

Mosey looked puzzled and said, "I never asked 'em."

We ordered two more beers with the hamburgers and sat looking around the place for familiar or interesting people.

The afternoon faded into dusk, and Mosey and I were still sitting there drinking beer. We made numerous trips to the dirty old rest room in the course of these events. I was beginning to notice that I was not walking in a very straight line when I made such trips. Mosey had befriended a slim, blond-haired girl and was trying to get me to tell some marine stories. I reminded him of The Laughing Man's show, and we took the blonde and a six-pack of beer and headed off across town on foot.

Mosey sang:

"Boys, don't go drinking and gambling,
It'll drag you all down into hell"

The little blond-haired girl said in a husky voice, "You gonna get into some trouble hollering up and down the streets."

By the time we reached the high school where The Laughing Man was performing, it was almost show-time, and we had to take a seat at the top of the bleachers. I remember standing up in the middle of the show and waving my arms. I remember laughing long after the others had stopped. I remember The Laughing Man looking angry from the stage. I remember a man in a blue coat with shiny buttons coming up the bleachers toward me. That's all I remember.

I woke up and looked around the jailhouse. It was a wide room with a huge metal door at one end and a large naked light bulb high in the center. There was a window set high in the wall at the other end of the room. There were four empty cells along the far side of the jail. There were several people sitting, standing, and sleeping in the room. I sat up and pulled the blanket around me. I was sick and frightened. No one spoke to me. I tried to remember more of what had happened, and I couldn't. I looked around the room for Mosey or the blonde. They were not there.

Presently one of the men sleeping on the floor awoke and looked at me. He didn't have a blanket. He came toward me and grabbed the corner of the blanket and jerked it from under me, causing my head to bang against the wall. I vomited. The ugly old man cursed me. "You son of a bitch, you took my goddamned blanket while I was asleep. I'll bust anybody's ass who takes my blanket, you cocksucker."

I wondered how much pain and misery a man must experience before he is allowed to die. I would gladly have died to be relieved of the pain and agony that I felt.

I scooted back up against the wall and put my head in my hands. I wanted to tear the pain out of my head with my fingers. I cried.

It seemed like hours before I got to my feet and walked to the other end of the room, away from the man from whom I had stolen the blanket. I stood near the window and tried to stretch tall enough to look out. There was no ledge under the window. Suddenly a man kicked a wooden box toward me. It frightened me. He said, "Stand on the box."

I stood on the box and looked out the window. There was a gray wall several feet away. You could not see up or down the alley. I stretched and saw the dirt of the ground beneath the window. I wanted out.

Occasionally a guard would unlock the huge metal door and call out someone's name. He came this time for Clyde Mitch. "Clyde Mitch" he yelled. Everyone looked at one another. "Clyde Mitch" he yelled again. We looked. He pointed the key ring at me and said, "You, boy, don't you know your own damned name?"

I looked behind me, but there was no one there. I pointed at myself, asking "You mean me?"

"Yes, *you*, dammit."

I walked to the door and he took me by the arm and led me up a flight of stairs to a large room with about fifteen people seated on wooden benches. There was a flag of some kind on a desk and a picture of Abraham Lincoln on the dirty wall. The guard shoved me down on a bench and took a seat by the door.

It was then that one man jumped to his feet and screamed at another, "You touch my wife again and I'll kill you, you son of a bitch!"

The guard jumped to his feet with a huge black nightstick in his hand and started beating one of the men. I could see the blood coming as I heard the stick connect with the man's skull. I thought, "My God, it'll kill him."

Then I thought I could smell the blood, so I got to my feet and started looking for a place to vomit again. I pushed open the door and went down a long hallway and walked out onto the streets of Middletown. I vomited alongside the building, walking as the hot white water splashed on the street. And then there was nothing left. I continued to walk and was several blocks away before I realized I had escaped from jail. I felt a sense of elation. How could a man be so elated and so sick?

I walked faster now. I asked a lady how to get to Route 52, and she said I was on it, but I was in the middle of town.

I caught a ride with an insurance salesman and arrived back in Woodmont Coves in the late afternoon.

I reflected on the name "Clyde Mitch" and knew where I had gotten it. I thought about the fact that I had no wallet and no identification. They would continue to look for a person named Clyde Mitch. I was broke.

As I slept in the late afternoon sun: "There it is, boy, the end of the world. What do you think now? Feel the edge of it. Ain't that smooth? It stops right here. See out there, down there, nothing but clear blue nothing. Who told you different?" The man who spoke pushed me and I fell, twisting to see the fat Laughing Man standing at the edge of the world, and I screamed.

Mitch had his hand in my hair and was shaking my head when I awoke. I looked at him and said, "Thank you."

Dr. John Friend sat in his easy chair watching his wife knit yet another something for charity. He reached down beside his chair and picked up the dark blue .38 caliber pistol. He checked to make sure it was loaded, pulled back the hammer and put the gun to his head. He moved his fingers ever so slightly. He took the gun from his temple and looked into the barrel. He perspired a little.

Mrs. John Friend put her knitting down and said, "John, I just wish you wouldn't do that. It makes me nervous, and one day you'll hurt yourself."

John laid the pistol by his chair. Mrs. Friend continued. "I just wish Dr. Carter had never told you about that dangerous practice as a form of therapy."

Dr. John Friend eased back into his chair and remarked, "Life is always in a very delicate balance. It is precious. It may well be that it is all we have or will ever have. When a person gets bored, he is wasting the most valuable thing in this universe, life. This practice gives me an appetite, it makes me thirsty, it makes me want to live, it makes me want to walk and breathe and move about. And so, with your permission, I believe I'll do all that. I'll be at the diner if anyone calls." And with that the good doctor walked up Hill Avenue to the Main Street Diner.

Dr. Friend walked into the diner and took a seat at the back of the room. He arranged his place setting into a neat display and drummed his fingers on the edge of the table.

Gloria Strong, a stunning red-haired girl with smooth, flawless skin and a pair of green fluttering eyes, walked toward the doctor's table. Her nose was slightly upturned, giving it a cutish look, and her mouth was wide and wet-looking. She made her way to the doctor's table, looked around the café to see if anyone could hear, and said, "Hi, honey."

Dr. Friend smiled his most professional smile and said, "Hi, how's my all-time favorite patient today?"

"Why, she's fine, thank you," Gloria Strong laughed.

Out of sight of the other customers, Dr. Friend patted her smooth, round leg. "I believe you're about ready for a checkup," he said.

Gloria Strong laughed again. "Why, I've just been feeling poorly, Mr. Doctor."

Gloria took the doctor's order. As she walked away toward the kitchen, the doctor remembered the first time he had gotten to know her.

It had been just after her graduation, and she had come to him for a checkup before going away to college. She had walked into the office with an air of confidence that he had seldom witnessed in a patient. She spoke, laughing about her checkup. "My mother, Lydia—you know Lydia Strong, don't you? Well, she said I should come down here and let you look me over. I almost told her you had looked me over plenty of times while I was a cheerleader."

Dr. Friend was a little surprised at her brassy attitude. She walked around the small office looking at framed articles on the wall, picking up small objects, all the while tossing her red hair.

Not knowing how familiar he should be with her, the doctor decided to be as professional as possible. "Would you sit on the examining table, please?"

Gloria Strong bounced lightly to the table. Dr. Friend said, "Did you bring the urine sample?"

She reached for her purse and produced a small bottle filled to the brim. He put away the small container and proceeded to do the ear, nose and throat examinations. He checked her eyes and took a blood sample, at which she winced, "Oooh. Now that pains me."

"Would you remove your underthings and lie back on the table please?"

He went to a corner of the room and made a few notes on a chart as she removed a pair of blue lace panties and placed them at the end of the table. He returned to find she had laid back on the table with her skirt already up. It was during the examination that she raised herself slowly from the table, placed her arms around his neck and kissed him. He walked to the door and locked it. He came back to the table, removed his trousers, and made slow, rhythmic love to Gloria Strong. He had made love to her in that fashion ever since.

Gloria never went away to college.

Dr. Friend was jarred out of his daydream by Gloria Strong's hand on his. She had slid into the booth beside him and was asking a question. "Did you bring your sweetheart patient her medicine?"

"The medicine is not available at this time."

Gloria jumped to her feet. "That's what you said yesterday. Look, no more checkups for this little lady until you get the pills for me."

"Look, I'm a doctor. Those things are dangerous in the quantities you take."

"You will not see me again, Doctor. I have friends who can get the same thing in Middletown. But you owe me."

"Look. Could you cut down a little, say, two a day?"

"That's easy for you to say; you don't have to work around this godforsaken place all the time. You know what it's like with a carnival in town? They've pinched my butt till it's blue."

"You're headed for detox at this rate. I can't let you do it."

"I could have a little chat with Mrs. John Friend."

They were talking in loud whispers, and the doctor

said, "Shhh. Look, I'll get you one hundred more pills. That's the end of it for me, and that will be the end of it for you. Is that a deal?"

Gloria tossed her red hair. "Today," she said.

Gloria Strong had once asked for something to keep her awake. The doctor had obliged.

I went to the shed behind my father's house and got my salve bag, an old army cloth bag with a shoulder strap. I picked up some clean clothes, went to the paint factory for a shower, and went out to sell some salve.

I sold most of the salve to people with children. My father had told almost all of his patients to rub a little salve on the chest of a sick child. It went quickly, so today I walked straight to the houses of people with children. I sold about eight dollars' worth in an hour and a half. It was standing talking to people that took up most of the time.

I had not eaten in twenty-four hours. I started toward the Main Street Diner. Dodd Givens yelled at me from the front of his store. I pretended not to hear him. He caught up with me as I was about to enter the diner. "James, are you losing your hearing?" he asked. "I want to buy a couple of cans of salve."

I took the salve bag off my shoulder and offered him two cans. He gave me the two dollars and thanked me. I said, "Mr. Givens, what do you do with so much salve?"

"Well, I uh . . . colds, we have a lot of colds. Thank you, James."

I went inside the Main Street Diner and saw my

father in some kind of earnest conversation with Gloria Strong. They didn't notice me, and so I took a seat at the front.

I wanted the carnival to leave town. I wanted the Strawberry Festival to end. I wanted Dr. Friedman's body laid away. And I wanted the peace and quiet, and even boredom, to replace the chaos of my life. It was not normal. Had I gone from being plain curious to being crazy?

The sixth day of the Strawberry Festival dawned clear and sunny. Although I had been instructed not to, I had spent the night in the Woodmont Coves First Methodist Church. I had slept sound and dream-free for about nine hours, and I had a feeling that I could get hold of everything if I could but relax for a while in my old place at the dealership.

I went to the bus station and found an almost new paperback book titled *Take the Fear from Your Life*. It read, in part:

Are you a failure in life? Is your marriage falling apart? Are you angered about the misfortune fate has handed you? Would you like to stand up, be counted, take charge of your life and your destiny once and for all? Try the plan that has worked for thousands. In this handy little book, Doctor . . .

I put the book in my pocket and walked toward the dealership. I could see Clyde and Mitch standing looking at something on the ground. As I drew close enough to see what they were interested in, I saw a small rabbit writhing on the ground. Clyde said, "Hit by a car."

I made a motion toward the rabbit, which had been injured in one of its back legs. Clyde held my arm and said, "They bite."

There was a sudden smacking sound as Mitch hit the rabbit across the back of the head with an iron pipe. The rabbit lay silent now, its fur slowly losing the shiny, smooth ruffle of a minute ago; it was sprawled out in the parking area like a piece of an old worn coat.

Clyde picked up the animal and carried it to the huge garbage bin by the shed and dropped it inside. His shoulders indicated that he sighed deeply before turning to come back to his place against the wall. "They're good to eat," he said.

Mitch began to cry. I walked down to my father's house, picked up my dirty clothes and walked back up the other side of the street to the laundromat.

I was sitting watching the monotonous gyrations of the washing apparatus through the window of the washing machine when the lady from the carnival came in. She was not wearing the black britches and white top she had worn the first night I had told her the marine story. She wore a large, loose, tentlike dress with black-and-orange flowers printed on it. She carried her clothes in a small plastic bag. She stood before the washing machine and stuffed her things into the washer, reached up under the long dress she wore and removed a pair of panties that she was wearing and dropped them inside the washer. She picked some coins from her purse and started the machine. She walked to where I was sitting and said, "You da marine, ain'tcha?"

"I'm not a marine," I confessed.

"I ain't sometin like no Maralyn Monroe, eder."

She looked at me for a minute and said, "What chu do?"

"I don't do much. I sell stuff."

"What chu sell?"

"Salve."

"Salve?"

"Yeah."

"You a cute boay. Mos boays tawk, tawk, tawk. You don tawk, tawk, tawk."

"I get tired."

"Me, too, me, too," she said. "Why don you come by my trailer at de hamburger place at de fair, and I'll cook you some good steak meat. Wat chu tink?"

"What time?"

"Bout leven tirty dis evenin'."

"I'll see, thank you."

"You be dere, you be glad, I cook good."

I was aware whe was not wearing her panties under the long dress, and I wondered about her. I realized then that I did not like boredom as much as I had thought.

I took my laundry bag and walked back to the dealership. Mitch was doing a monologue on nature:

"Now you take dat bluebird, he smart and he cool to fly so low and sweet and sing too. He make da mornin' cool and de sky blue and da little furry guys like him some also you can bet. I say, Hoo Hoo Hoo to you bluebird. Ain't dat sumptin' ridin' down at road for some lonesome reason, you hear. I said let her go and don worry none anyway."

I put the laundry bag under my head, lay back to read my book and slept and dreamed:

The Doctor Who Hated Fear came rolling up in a huge truck. He stepped from the cab and was eight feet tall. He walked over to Mitch and Clyde and shaved them and cut their hair. He dressed them in tuxedoes and gave them each a cigar and an easy chair made of fine leather. He clothed me in a blue suit, maroon tie, and a blue shirt. He touched my head where I had banged it against the jailhouse wall and the soreness went away. He drove his truck to Maude Primm's apartment, knocked the lock off the freezer, and took Dr. Friedman's body to a beautiful spot in the cemetery and sang:

Ahhhhhh Meeeeen

The Doctor Who Hated Fear went to my father's office and stocked it with all-new shiny equipment. He built a huge building behind my father's house, and it was a hospital. He waved his hand at my mother and she became young and wore a pretty hat with flowers. He drove to Middletown and saved the life and sanity of Joe Morgan and gave him a new truck. He found Gloria Strong and sent her away to a fine girls' school. He waved his hand and the Strawberry Festival disappeared. He waved his hand again and Windfield Waycross gave everyone some jewelry. He brought Claudia Barnes back to life, and she waved good-bye to two of her husbands.

The Doctor Who Hated Fear stood on the sidewalk and wiped the sweat from his brow. "I told you I could do it," he said in a loud, clear voice.

I applauded him and said, "What do we do now?"

The Doctor Who Hated Fear rubbed his chin, took a deep breath and said, "I don't know. I don't know."

I awoke to find that Mitch and Clyde had gone down to the liquor store without me.

I took my laundry bag and put my clean clothes in the shed behind my father's house. I met Mitch and Clyde coming up the street from the liquor store. I had never met them on a sidewalk before, and we didn't know what to do or say to one another. I bowed slightly, Clyde grunted something, and Mitch and I looked back at one another when we had passed. They were carrying some small brown bags.

I knew I didn't want to go to see the lady at the hamburger stand at the carnival. I walked across Second Street to the liquor store and waited while the old, stooped man who ran the place did something to a small piece of accounting equipment. He put some paper into it and rattled off a few numbers on the machine and threw the scrap of paper into a wastebasket. "Help you?" he asked.

"Er . . . ah . . . Is there any reason sloe gin would give a person a headache?"

The old man scratched the side of his gray face and thought a second, then he said, "Well, might be too sweet."

"What ain't too sweet?"

"Never drank a drop in my life . . . wouldn't know . . . just know what they tell me. I sell a lot of vodka."

"Well, I'll take a small vodka."

"Pint, half pint?"

"Uh, pint . . . pint."

The old man put the bottle, wrapped in a brown bag, on the counter and took my money. While he was making change, I opened the bottle and smelled it. He came back with the change and said quickly, "You can't open that in here."

"Sorry."

"That's a different law. You have to have another license to open bottles on the premises."

"It smells awfully dry."

"I wouldn't know about that," he said, looking through the huge glass window of the place as if he were expecting someone to walk in or drive up.

I mumbled a thank you and walked out onto the sidewalk. It was late afternoon in Woodmont Coves.

I wanted to go over to the Boo River and sit for a while, so I walked up Market Street and went around behind Strong's Supermarket. There was a big flat rock that protruded into the water's edge, and that's where I positioned myself to watch the river flow lazily by. The sun filtered through the branches of the trees, and the rays of sunlight made a shimmering pattern on the slow-moving water. I thought of the underwater world of the fish, the worms, the bugs, the snakes, the eels, and the hundreds of other species that lived and died, preyed and ran, in the apparently calm and peaceful river. It seemed fair and equal for it to be that way.

I took a long drink of the vodka. For a second I was nauseated and choked by the bitter, burning taste. I didn't like vodka, and I almost threw the remaining colorless liquid into the river. I sat very quietly for a minute or two, and soon the calm euphoria that I had experienced before came over me, and I laughed a little laugh and said something to the rock on which I sat.

A huge bass glided back over its spawning place. A smooth bed of sand about two feet in diameter outlined the beautiful fish—as if it were mounted and framed.

I lay on my stomach and watched the slight movement of the fish. Without any apparent effort it glided slowly around the small bed of sand, expressionless, of course, and yet somehow defiant and watchful.

I sat upright as footsteps on the riverbank became louder. I looked to see Dodd Givens coming down the river with a fishing pole in his hand.

I spoke to Mr. Givens. "Afternoon, Mr. Givens."

"Howdy, James. Fishing?"

"Naw, I was just sitting here thinking about something."

Dodd Givens came out onto the rock and stood above me. "It don't pay to fish this time of year. The fish are spawning, and they won't bite."

"I know."

He reached into his jacket pocket and took out a brown bottle of whiskey. "Mind if I sit down and have a drink with you?"

"Not at all," I said.

We sat and talked about Woodmont Coves for the better part of an hour. It was getting dark when Dodd Givens proposed that we have some fun. "Did you ever go the regional fair in Middletown, James?"

"No, sir."

"Well, I used to be real big in the 4-H Club in high

school, and we used to go over there and enter some of our animals in the competition. Used to sleep in the barns and live on the fairgrounds for a week at a time. I guess that was the most fun I ever had. I caught the pig in the greasy pig contest two years in a row; beat out a lot of football and basketball players, too. They never let me play sports in high school; said I was too clumsy."

He sat with a faraway look in his eyes as he related his adventures. "See, what they would do is grease this pig and turn it loose in one of the holding pens. We'd all get in there and try to catch it. Whoever caught it got a cash prize and they got to take the pig home to boot. Balance is the secret of it. If you can balance him somehow, you pretty much got him. You can't hold onto him, though; it's balance, that's the trick. I never told anybody else, but it's balance."

I could tell we were both getting drunk. I had finished almost half of my vodka, and Dodd Givens had finished his bottle completely and thrown it into the river. He stood and made the motion of holding a greased pig in his arms as he spoke. "Balance," he said.

We went over to Mr. Givens' house to see his pig. It was standing in a little pen in the corner of his back lawn where he had built a six-foot-high redwood fence. A tall person would have to stand on tiptoe to look into his back lawn. Mr. Givens went into his kitchen and came back with the two cans of salve I had sold him. He went over to where the little pig was penned up and reached over and started to rub the salve all over the little creature. "Now, this salve is the best stuff in the

world for this sport. If he happens to run into something and bruises or cuts himself in any way, he's
already coated with this stuff, and he heals right up. I
would have recommended it to the fair officials if I had
thought of it then." Mr. Givens went into the kitchen
and washed his hands; he came back out dressed in a
gray cotton sweatsuit. "You wanna try him first, or you
want me to show you how balance works?" he asked.

"Naw, I don't wanna try him."

Mr. Givens opened the gate to the little pen and
turned the pig loose in his back lawn. He made a jumping motion toward the pig, and it lurched forward in a
short run. He pursued the pig in earnest now. It
twisted and turned and evaded his every effort to scoop
it into his arms. He was laughing loudly and yelling for
me to join him in the chase. The pig came near the
porch where I was sitting, and I made a grab for it. The
pig easily slipped through my arms and I found myself
covered with salve and face down in the grass. I jumped
to my feet and let out a sort of cowboy whoop and
took off across the lawn after the small animal. I missed
the pig once and collided with the redwood fence,
scraping the side of my face on the rough wood. The
pig stood defiantly and warily in the corner of the lawn
when Mrs. Givens appeared on the kitchen porch. She
spoke loudly. "Dodd, you two are attracting the attention of everyone in the neighborhood, and your dinner
is almost ready. Come in and wash up and change
clothes."

Dodd Givens lay breathless and greasy on the grass.
He looked over at me sitting exhausted near him. He

ignored his wife and spoke to me. "Maybe we had too much kickapoo joy juice, James." He laughed loudly and got to his feet.

I walked to the gate where we had entered the back lawn and turned and spoke to Dodd Givens. "Thank you, thank you. It is a great sport."

Mrs. Givens looked at me disapprovingly and went back into the kitchen. I closed the gate behind me and became aware of the terrible odor of the salve. I rubbed the side of my face and realized that I was bleeding slightly.

I started toward the carnival grounds and the hamburger stand, smelling terrible and feeling tired and happy.

I sat on an old wooden crate beside a darkened tent and watched the girl in the black britches and white top cook hamburgers. I waited and sipped on my vodka. As I sat in the darkness, I watched the people of Woodmont Coves and surrounding rural areas walk wearily by. They seemed bored and broke. I wondered why they came to these places and could not find the true answer—if there was one.

The vodka was almost all gone when The Hamburger Girl tied down the flap on the concession stand for the night. I walked around behind the tent where her trailer was parked and said, "Hi, I'm your marine friend."

"Go in da trailer and wait," she said.

I sat on a small sofa by the kitchen table and looked around the small enclosure. It was gypsylike in appearance. There were bright colors all around, and even in the soft light the place reminded me of the black-and-orange dress that she had worn at the laundromat. There was a sweet smell in the air.

The first words she uttered when she entered the trailer were, "My goodness, wat's dat awful smell in heah?"

She came to where I sat and took hold of my arm. "Wat on earth iz you been into, boay? Get up heah and let me look atch."

"It was an accident," I said.

"Wat is it?"

"Salve."

"Well, get up to da sink and warch it off."

She handed me a small towel and a bar of soap and turned on the water in the small sink. She touched my arm and said, "You got dat stuff all ober yore close. Get out of em rite now."

I stepped to the back of the small trailer and took off my shirt. I started to take off my pants and I stopped. She came toward me and unzipped my fly and started pulling down my pants. She noticed that I was getting an erection. "Now, you ain't gonna need dat toy for a while, we gonna eat first."

When I was undressed she handed me the black-and-orange dress and said, "Slip id on for de time being."

I stood looking down at myself in the black-and-orange dress. The Hamburger Girl kicked my shoes under the sofa and took my shirt and pants outside and dropped them on the ground beside the trailer. "Dat stuff smells awful, an' me cookin' a steak," she said.

I sat on the small sofa in my dress and could smell

the steaks cooking on the grill of the hamburger concession. When I smelled the food, I realized how hungry I was.

The Hamburger Girl chatted constantly as she prepared the meal. We had a baked potato, steak, a salad,
and a sweet drink that she mixed in tall green glasses.
We had sex twice that night, and I had only to pull the
black-and-orange dress above my waist to participate.

The Hamburger Girl was shaking me, speaking to
me, when I awoke. "Somebody, one a dese damm car-
neys, has stole yo clothes in de nite. You betta get up
and get outa here fore de pebbles get movin' roun.'"

She handed me my shoes and my socks and busied
herself putting away the dishes from our dinner of the
night before. I sat on the bed and put on my shoes and
socks. I let the information that my clothes had been
stolen sink in. "They've stolen my clothes?"

"Dey stole yo clothes. Deyed steal yo shit if you
didn't have a toilet."

"Well, I . . ."

"Jus git outa heah rite now, and you can brang de
dress back later. Now git."

"Yeah . . . okay."

I stumbled out into the early-morning light and
started across the fairgrounds to the back side of Hill
Avenue. No one spoke to me, although several of the
carnival workers were up and readying their stands for
the day's activities. I made my way around behind the
laundromat and down behind the dealership to see if
Mitch and Clyde were out. They sat dozing in their
customary place, so I hurried past without looking in

their direction. I made it to the shed to find my clothes. With my adrenaline flowing and the vodka still in my system, I began to feel brave. I gathered some clothes from the shed and marched off to the paint factory in the black-and-orange dress.

The guard at the paint factory jumped to his feet as I walked hurriedly by him. "Hey! James Friend?"

He stood with his hands on his hips. "You joined up with Willie Alexander and them boys?"

"No, it was an accident." I turned and kept on walking. I could hear the guard talking to me, but I kept on walking to the fluffy white towels and the steaming sanctuary of the redwood shower stalls.

The Strawberry Festival left Woodmont Coves in a swift, sad day and night. The Ferris wheel was gone. Then tents and trucks moved away during the night, and the ladies' decorating committee, of which my mother was a member, took down the huge red strawberries that adorned the windows of the shops and public buildings.

It had been a good distraction. I knew that now. The townspeople were saying they weren't sure they would have another festival. They were tired and complained about the revenue not being as much as was predicted. Woodmont Coves had been a different town during the festival. It was like ending a vacation and yet not packing and leaving the vacation site. It was as if the vacation site had left the town. We have put on a show for the people who came to put on a show for us, and we were all tired of the posture we had struck and had settled back into our casual slump of a disposition. The townspeople walked a little slower, the anxiety was gone, the show was over, and the show was gone. The carnival people were miles away, rolling to yet another town with the belief that they knew the people in Woodmont Coves, which, of course, they didn't.

 Jimmy Barrett leaned his stocky, five-eleven frame against his police car, ran his hand through his short blond hair and said to no one in particular, "Now we can be about our regular business."

He adjusted the police paraphernalia around his waist and struck his favorite military pose. He looked up and down Main Street, put his hand behind his head to rub his neck and yawned.

Mayor Arthur Lovette sat at his desk on the second floor of the courthouse and leafed through a manila folder marked "Strawberry Festival." There were insurance forms, lease agreements and various papers dealing with the festival. There was a small yellow check in the amount of $643.22. There was a picture of a clown bursting through the head of a marching drum in the upper-left-hand corner of the check, and he tried to remember if he had seen a clown at the carnival; he was sure he had not. He touched a button on his desk that would summon his secretary and close the file on the Strawberry Festival for another year.

From the window above her kitchen sink Mrs. John Friend could see apples beginning to take form on the small tree in the backyard. Her mother had named her Buffet. She had wanted her to have a French name. It was a source of embarrassment to her. She had never dreamed of being a doctor's wife. She had been pretty. When John Friend had proposed to her, he was an intern at the big hospital in Cincinnati. When she had told her parents that she was going to marry a doctor, they were overjoyed. It was as if she were going to marry a king.

Although she was from a poor family, John Friend had assured her that it did not matter. However, he was sometimes alarmed to see her parents, her two sisters, and her three brothers tramping through the hospital looking for him to pay a friendly visit. The visitors were ill-clothed and not well mannered. It was not until Dr. Friend's family had moved away to Woodmont Coves to open his first practice that the visits stopped.

Buffet Friend stood at her kitchen sink and thought back over the past twenty-two years. She had made every effort to be a good doctor's wife. But even after all these years someone would occasionally ask her how things were in Cincinnati. She would forever remain an outsider to the old families in Woodmont Coves.

The hot water from the sink was running over onto her feet. Mrs. Friend jumped back, grabbed the faucet handle and turned the water off. She shook herself back to the present and reached for a mop that was leaning between the sink and the stove in the small kitchen. She finished mopping the floor around the sink and wiped her brow with a freckled hand. Her red-gray hair was in disarray and her feet were wet. Her small, round features conveying despair, she huddled in a chair in the kitchen and cried for the first time in a long while. Her husband came into the kitchen for another cup of coffee and saw her sitting there crying. "Did you let the sink run over again? Did you take your medicine?"

"John, the medicine has started to make me have nightmares. You would not believe some of the things that I dream. I feel better in the daytime, but I can't face the night and the dreams. Isn't there something else I could take?"

"The dreams are only dreams. Once you realize that you'll feel better about them, and they will eventually go away. It's a side effect of the medicine, but it does relieve the depression, doesn't it?"

"Yes, but maybe I should get off it for a while, maybe I should get out and do something. I don't do very much, you know."

"You worked your tail off on the Strawberry Festival. I call that doing something."

"That was a failure, too."

"Maybe you should go to Cincinnati and see your folks. You know they love to see you."

"Mama's dead and Daddy's drinking so since she passed away. It depresses me even more to see them all in such straits. Why don't we build that new house?"

"I don't want to talk about a new house. I wouldn't live on Second Street in one of those big houses if they gave me one. We'd rattle around in it like gravel in a tin can. This place is plenty big."

Buffet Friend stared at her hands. She had been wringing them until they were red and bloody-looking. "I haven't heard from James," she lamented.

"He had to move out of his trailer for the festival. I'd say you'll hear from him soon."

John Friend did not mention to his wife that he had seen their son behind their house wearing a black-and-orange dress. He had stood behind the door as his son had gathered clean clothes from the shed and had marched off with such arrogance in such ridiculous garb.

Buffet Friend stood and raised herself to her full height and announced, "Well, I'm going to stay off the medicine for a few days and see how I feel. I'm going to make some new curtains for this window. They look drab against the pretty weather. I will hear from James, won't I?"

"You will hear from James," he said.

Dear Mother,

You wouldn't dream of all the fun I had during the Strawberry Festival. It's the first time I realized how much work you and the other members of the other committees do. I met some very nice people from the carnival. One of them was a very good cook.

I know you have been concerned about some of my activities. I have been out of my trailer and have not had access to my typewriter. Salve sales are up.

I went to Middletown to see The Laughing Man and met a nice young man named Mose. I forget his last name, but he was a good person and was industrious and knew father.

Are there plans for another festival next year?

You know people are very tired every year after the festival and say they won't do it again, but they always do, don't they?

When do you think you and father will begin work on your new house? You know how much that house means to you, and I can't wait for you to get started. You love to plan and organize anyway.

Mother, I have not been a very exemplary son, and I know that. You have my heartfelt apology for the heartache that I have caused you. I feel bad about it and look for new ways to make amends and to deserve the love and affection that you have always shown for me. We are young, and the time will come when you will be proud of me, you will see. I will find that niche and do that thing which you have always wanted someone in the family to do. Maybe I will travel some. I'm not sure just yet about any of it and will let you know if I have, or make, any firm plans. Would it please you if I were a marine? I have asked a few people about it, and they have intimated to me that they think I would make a good one.

My weight is down a little, I think. It is probably from all the activity during the festival.

I am making some hard, definite plans now, and you will soon have some news of some kind. I don't want you to feel anxious about any of it, but I am excited about some things, and I'll let you know. Okay?

All other statements that I have made can now be set aside for this one: I love you, respect you, and wish you all the best.

And with that, dear Mother, I close my letter reporting on my excellent health and my intention to be your loyal, loving and industrious son.

As always,

Your son, James

The fat lady who ran the milk bottle game at the carnival and the man who owned the Ferris wheel left my trailer far cleaner than it was when they moved in. It fairly shined. I guess this was a practice to keep them in the good graces of the community year after year. All of my things were arranged neatly in place, pretty much where I had left them. There was a small jar of buttons, safety pins, nails, and things of that sort sitting on the small dining table where I had left it. A picture of The Laughing Man was still pinned above the mirror in the small bathroom. It was good to be back in the trailer. The old lady who ran the trailer park came ambling by, peered into the window to see me sitting on the bed, and went on about her business. I was officially home now. I sang a song:

> "Claudia Barnes, Claudia Barnes
> Had three husbands and a farm
> Raised the hay and sold the hay
> Morgan shot her by the way"

I sat on the edge of my bed in the trailer and ate a can of cold peas that had been left in the cupboard. I ate all I could get out with the spoon and then held the can up to my lips and drank the remaining juice. I threw the container into the small trash can by the stove and contemplated my career in the marines:

All right men. This is the marines. You will behave like men. Any man here who thinks he's tougher than me will fall out and prove it. You will have your stuff shiny at all times. You will probably be killed in the line of duty in some strange country, but don't worry; that is the life of a marine. Don't worry about your parents. Any man who gets homesick will be kicked out of this movie. You got that?

I postponed my plans to enlist in the marines for a while, got up and walked down to the dealership to check on Mitch and Clyde.

I found Mitch and Clyde in their customary places, enjoying the early-morning sun. I sat down without saying a word. Staring off into the clear-blue sky, I could see a hawk circling slowly above a field to the west of town. I watched the hawk for ten to fifteen minutes, fighting off sleep. I had slept well and dream-free the night before, and something in me wanted to move around and do something. Nothing came to me that I felt I could easily accomplish. There was a slow murmur of traffic around town, and I got the impression that it was growing. The people might have been as restless as I.

No matter how hard I fought the drowsy feeling, it soon overpowered or tranquilized me, and I saw The Doctor Who Hated Fear drive up on the side of the street.

"I have come to put everything back as it was," he said. "It was just as well the way it was, so I've come to undo what I have done."

I looked at him and said, "There is no need for all that fuss. We know now that you were only a dream."

"Ah, there is the problem all around and in and out. You think it doesn't matter to us people who live in dreams. You believe that everything is real and that we have no feelings. Well, let me assure you that you will live as much or more of your life in my dimension as you will in yours. Do you not know the difference between planning and executing? Do you not know the difference between wanting and having? Can't you see that over half your life is thinking? Acting! The secret to success and happiness is acting. Oh, very well," said the eight-foot Doctor Who Hated Fear, "you shall have it as you shall have it. I will leave things as I put them here in this dream, but remember that you will have to contend with it."

The Doctor Who Hated Fear climbed into his truck and shouted out the window, "How are you enjoying life in the marines?" He laughed a hearty, good-natured laugh, waved, and flew away in his vehicle. A sign on the side of the flying truck read:

THE MARINES IS FOR YOU

I awoke and found myself standing. I looked down at Clyde, who was watching me, and said, "Have you ever been in the marines?"

Clyde shook his head from side to side and said, "No, the Army."

I was afraid, excited, and I had a hurting headache.

"James?" It was the voice of Clyde. "Sit down a minute."

I sat down against the wall and put my arm on the concrete block. I was not expecting the lecture that followed.

"James, you are a man now. You are growing up. This is not the life for a young man."

Clyde rubbed his scraggly old stubbly face and tried to smile. Had I seen him smile before?

"Go on," he said. "Really."

I didn't like him talking so much. Had I been talking too? I sat silently and looked at the gravel in the parking lot. I realized that it was not Woodmont Coves that was growing; it was me. Every noise seemed to notify me of some impending event that would catch me up and carry me off into some responsibility. I didn't want it. I could bear the silence no longer. I stared straight ahead and said, "Thank you."

I jumped to my feet and went quickly around the corner of the dealership and walked to my trailer. I sat on the small bed and wondered how much I had left unsaid in my short life. Should I have said more? I tried to remember.

I looked back over the brief years. I had never told my father or mother that I loved them. They had never said they loved me—in so many words. Maybe I was an unwanted child. Perhaps I was an accidental child. It didn't seem feasible with my father being a doctor. I had never felt threatened or insecure. There was very little that could happen to a young child in a small, conservative town like Woodmont Coves. I wondered about other children's lives and realized that I knew little or nothing about what their lives were really like. Maybe I was normal.

I started a process of thinking that should not have started. It was too busy; it was complicated; it was not comforting.

I firmed my jaw and rationalized that I was not to blame for anything. I did not kill Dr. Friedman . . . I did not steal his body . . . I did not . . . I started humming. I grabbed my head and stood up. I must not start humming; that will not help. I was panicky. I sang:

"From this valley they say you are going . . ."

I stopped when I heard a knock on the door. "Yes?"

The knocking continued. I opened the door and saw my old landlady standing there. "Yes?" I said.

"Turn your porch light off; light bills are high."

"Yes, I'll do that. I'll turn off the light."

I flipped off the porch light switch and began to sing:

"Light bills are high in the valley
They're high in the valley all right
The light bills are high in the valley . . ."

The old lady moved across the trailer park with her shawl about her shoulders, stopping to pick up a piece of paper. I thought of several ways I could kill her.

When I awakened in the morning I was quiet for a few minutes. I was calm and clearheaded. I dressed and walked down Hill Avenue on the side of the street opposite Mitch and Clyde. I walked to the front of my father's house and sat down across the street on the little slope of grass. I sat there, feeling better, for about an hour. My father came walking down Hill Avenue toward me. He got close enough to speak and said, "Come on over."

He walked across the street, looked back, and left the door to his office open as he entered.

I walked across the street and stood in the open doorway. "How's Mother?"

"She's fine. I had breakfast at the diner; I got up early this morning. How are you?"

"I'm not sure. Could I talk to you?"

"Sure, what's on your mind?"

I was surprised to hear myself laughing a small laugh. "Uh, that's what I want to talk to you about."

"Shoot."

I felt better now that I had someone to talk with. I sat down on the small wooden chair by the door and said, "I've been afraid of something, but I don't know what it is."

My father sat rubbing his pocket watch with his thumb. He said, "Go on."

"I don't know what it is. I'm sad, very sad, for nothing."

I looked up to see my father looking very troubled. Gaining his composure, he said, "More."

"That's it. I just feel sad and funny." My father waited for me to go on. "I've thought some crazy things."

"Such as?"

"I thought of killing the old lady who runs the trailer park."

My father walked to the doorway and looked out into the street. He asked, "What did she do to you?"

"Oh, no. She's a lady, a real nice lady. I just said it was a crazy thought. She hasn't done anything to me. It was just a thought of some kind."

My father sighed a deep sigh. He turned and walked back to his desk and sat on the edge of it. Looking at the wall, he began to speak. "A lot of people have come in here with this same problem in the last few days. I think it must be post-festival depression, if there's a name for it. We get so excited about this damned festival every year that we forget our normal routines and our normal habits. I think the whole town suffers because of this thing. I have to deal with the anxiety before and the depression afterward."

I sat silently, feeling better. My father continued. "James, do you know what 'normal' is? No need to answer that. Normal is the sun coming up and the sun going down. Normal is summer, winter, spring, and fall. Normal is boys and girls. Normal is water and wind. You understand?"

"Yes, sir."

"Well, now you see we have a little bit of logic going here. Anything that fits outside this logic that we have is abnormal. Now, don't let that alarm you. There are not many normal things in the world. It might be a good idea to kill your landlady. In the society in which we live, within the rules as we know and understand them, it is not a good idea to kill your landlady. You follow me?"

"Yes, sir."

"Then I'll shut up. People don't remember long speeches."

He reached into his pocket and handed me a bottle

of small yellow pills. "Take one of these now and another when you feel the need."

"Are they bad for me?"

"Coffee is bad for you. Coke is bad for you. Food can be, too. It's up to you."

"Will they make me sick?"

"They differ; you'll know."

"Do I have to take them?"

"Do you want to kill your landlady? No, wait, that's not right. Look, I'm a doctor and that's medicine. I take six of them a day."

"Six?"

My father looked at me as if I were some grand inquisitor. "Six," he said. "Six."

My father gave me a glass of water, and I took one of the bitter-tasting pills. He looked out the door to the pretty summertime outside. "You know, James, I once thought of killing someone. But it was a long time ago."

I had a feeling the last sentence was added hastily. I mumbled a thank you and, feeling my old self again, walked back toward my trailer. I wondered if my mother took the same kind of pills.

I spent three days sleeping, reading and enjoying my newfound friends—the little yellow pills. I would awaken in the morning, take one of the pills and lie back for another nap. On the third day I didn't take the medicine. I gathered up some fresh clothes, went for a shower at the paint factory and stopped by to check on Mitch and Clyde. I sat down near the concrete block against the wall. I had found a newspaper to read. It was several days old, so I just read the classified ads. We had been sitting speechless for over an hour when Clyde got to his feet and stretched his old frame. He walked out to the edge of the street and looked up and down Hill Avenue. Mitch rolled over on his stomach and got to his feet by way of his hands and knees. I stood and leaned against the wall. Clyde motioned us out to the sidewalk with his head. We walked toward him as he started down Hill Avenue.

I walked behind Clyde and Mitch, down toward Second Street and the liquor store. When we reached Second Street, Clyde kept on walking and Mitch and I followed his lead. We crossed the avenue, past my father's house, and walked down Third Street to Strong's Supermarket. Clyde motioned for us to wait outside. He walked up and down the aisles of the market, and we could see him through the window. He came back with a grocery bag filled with frankfurters, mustard, soft drinks and potato chips. We walked around behind Strong's Supermarket to the big flat rock that stuck out into the river. Clyde found a handful of dry twigs and built a small fire in the middle of the rock. He put some larger pieces of wood on the little flames, and we soon had a nice weenie-roasting fire. He used his knife to cut some small, straight sticks from one of the overhanging limbs. We sat and roasted franks over the fire and drank bottles of cold grape soda and ate.

We sat cross-legged, away from the fire, which seemed hotter than usual because of the warm weather.

Jimmy Barrett came through the weeds and bushes to within twenty-five yards of where we sat. He stood there adjusting the police gear around his waist. He stood looking at us for a few minutes before saying, "When you boys get through with that picnic, be sure you kick that fire into the river. It's been awful dry around here, and we don't need to get a fire started." He took his sunglasses from a leather case on his belt, placed them on his nose and touched them with his index finger. He adjusted his hat and turned to walk back toward the market.

Mitch wiped his mouth on his sleeve, took a drink of the grape soda, and said loudly to no one in particular, "PO-LEECE!"

It was the only word spoken between us all day. We gathered our trash in the grocery sack, kicked the remaining pieces of burning wood into the Boo River and walked back to the dealership.

I stopped taking the pills after the third day. I didn't seem to need them. I was developing an appetite for food that I had never had before. I envisioned the steaks The Hamburger Girl had fixed for me. I could smell the sweet sizzle of fat in the fire. I could see the huge potato wrapped in foil and steaming on the plate. I could taste the brown, crispy piece of bread that we had eaten. I could find nothing in the trailer to eat. The carnival people had left a few cans of beans and peas behind, but I had eaten them my first few days back in the place, and now there was nothing.

I walked down toward Maude Primm's apartment, not really knowing I was going there. Somehow the taste of hot chicken noodle soup drew me. I stood against the wall of the place for a few minutes. I started rubbing the top of my head while I waited. I discovered that the top of my head was sore, as if I had hit it against something. I moved the skin on my head back and forth, feeling the soreness. I was surprised and a little frightened to discover that while I had been under the extreme pressure of my depression my scalp had been tingling.

Maude Primm never showed up at her apartment that afternoon; so I went back to my trailer and got my salve bag from under the bed. I started out on my usual route up Hill Avenue and out on River Road to sell some salve.

It was pleasant walking. The road was warm and shining in the hot sun, and I strayed to the side of it in the shade of the trees. There was a farmhouse back from the road about two hundred yards, and several children played around the front of the house as I walked to where they could see me. I asked one of the children if their mother was at home. They pointed to a garden spot some fifty yards away where a woman was hoeing in some vegetables. I walked over to where she was working and said hello.

"Hello, James." She wiped her hands on her apron. "I don't need any salve now; the kids just seem to get along fine in this warm weather."

Although most people called me by my first name, I knew very few of the people to whom I sold the salve.

I adjusted the salve bag on my shoulder and said, "Well, that's okay. I'll come back sometime when you think you need some."

The lady gardener came toward me through the

vegetable patch. "Are you going back into town?" she asked.

"No. I guess I'll go on out around the ridge to see if anybody needs some salve. I haven't sold any lately."

"I've baked some pies for Reverend Turner's bake sale tonight, and Henry's not gonna be here to take 'em over for me, and I thought you might."

"Maybe I could stop and get them on the way back in," I said.

"How long you gonna be?"

I looked back to the main road and thought of the hot, dusty walk around River Road and the trip back. I looked back at the lady gardener and said, "I guess I could take them in for you now. People won't want much salve this time of year."

"Now don't put yourself out," she said.

"No, no, that'll be okay. I'll take them in for you."

I ate one of the apple pies on the way back to town. I carried them for a good distance before looking inside the wax-paper wrapping to see what they were. The crust was warm and flaky, and the apples were still warm in the flaky shell. I ate one whole pie without giving it much thought.

I handed the other two pies to one of the ladies at the church and said, "The lady who lives on the left, back off River Road, sent these pies in for Reverend Turner. She said to give them to him."

One of the ladies took the pies and said, "You mean Mrs. Frensley?"

"I don't know her name, but I think that's it. She lives in the green house on the left, back off the road."

"That's Mrs. Frensley. I thought she was going to send three apples."

"Three apples?"

"Three apple pies. We thought she was sending three."

I pretended not to know anything and turned and walked down the street with my heart pounding.

I would lie about it. Three apples? What was this about three apples? I didn't see any apples at all. I was not told to bring any apples to the church. What did three apples have to do with it? They would probably say again that they were talking about three apple pies, but I would get confused and say that I didn't know what kind of pies they were and was not sure what had happened, especially to the apples. You see, I wouldn't have any way of knowing what kind of pies they were and so when they asked me about the pie that I had eaten, I would say that I didn't understand anything except that I had delivered something to church for some lady I didn't even know. And if there was a pie missing, I would be glad to pay for it as soon as I had sold some salve. I would also say that I had set the package down for a few minutes to get a rock out of my shoe, and maybe someone or something had gotten one of the pies, if that was what was in the package that I delivered.

I stood on the street corner to see if anyone walked toward the police station. I waited to see if there was any commotion around the church. I went back to my trailer and waited for someone to knock on my door. No one did.

I sat on the bed for a few minutes before reaching for my bottle of small yellow pills.

It was several uneventful days later, while sitting with Mitch and Clyde at the dealership, that I saw Mrs. Frensley coming toward me. I stood up and tried to form the answer to the question of the missing pie in my head. She had something in her hand as she spoke. "James, I wanted to thank you for delivering my pies to Reverend Turner the other day. Henry brought me in to do some shopping, and I had baked this pie for you. The bake sale was a big success, and they said that my pies were the ones that sold first. I can't thank you enough for helping me to do the Lord's work."

I took the pie from her and waited for her to mention the missing pie at the bake sale. She looked disapprovingly at Mitch and Clyde and said, "Well, I sure do appreciate it."

I looked at the pie, which was wrapped in wax paper, and said, "Uh, I don't like apple pie."

"Oh, that's not apple; that's cherry. It's fresh, and it came out real nice." Her husband was tooting the horn on the car. She made a motion to pat my shoulder and turned and went to the car.

Clyde looked up at me standing and holding the pie. "You don't like apple pie?" he asked.

"Well, I like cherry better."

We divided the pie in three pieces, and I ate mine in a flood of relief and guilt.

Clyde died.

It was two weeks past the Strawberry Festival and

we had had several rainy days in a row. Mitch and Clyde had spent a good deal of their time inside the shed where they lived. Mitch had come running to my trailer and had banged on the door until I was awake. I had never seen him in the trailer park and I was immediately alarmed when I saw him standing at my door. He didn't speak; he only motioned for me to follow him and went hobbling back toward the dealership. I put my clothes on as quickly as possible and ran past him when I had decided where he was going. Clyde was lying face up with his hands on his chest. He had turned blue. I ran to where he was lying and guessed what had happened. Mitch stood helplessly by and rubbed his hands up and down on the front of his legs. There was a pained expression on Mitch's face, and I worried for a moment that he, too, might have a stroke or heart attack. I put my head on Clyde's chest and listened for a heartbeat. I tried to remember how to take his pulse. Was it the thumb or finger? I could find no trace of life. I sat back on the gravel and looked at the peaceful blue face of my old friend. Mitch sat down beside me and sat staring at Clyde as if he were some curious thing that had been washed ashore in a flood. He seemed to expect Clyde to move or say something at any moment. He waited.

The rain had stopped and the dark, stringy clouds that had brought the rain the past few days were strung out in thin white and gray lines and were blowing toward the south. I watched their movement for a few minutes as if in a trance. "Was Clyde riding along on one of those clouds?" I wondered. Mitch raised his head and looked at the clouds as if he, too, thought the same thing. We sat and watched the spirit of our departed friend sail through the summer morning sky and resigned ourselves to the fact that he was gone. Gone forever and forever and forever.

"As blue as a grape," I thought. I put my head on his chest again, and it was colder this time. His face was cold, and his hands were clenched together. I tried to pull the fingers out of the grip and could not. I spoke to Clyde as if he were alive and yet I knew he was dead. "Where did you go, Clyde? What's it like out there? How did you get out so fast?"

I suddenly realized that I was not qualified to pronounce Clyde officially dead, and I ran to the police station and courthouse to find Jimmy Barrett. He was sitting in his police car in front of the building when I ran up to him. "I don't know if I'm supposed to tell you or somebody else, but I think Clyde's dead."

Jimmy Barrett started running toward the dealership, and I followed behind even though I could have outrun him. A sense of responsibility came over me, and I was not sure that I wanted to be involved in anyone's death no matter how close we were. I started trying to explain away my involvement as we ran. "He just lived over here all the time by the dealership, and I saw him every once in a while, but Mitch came to get me and that's all I know about it really."

Jimmy Barrett was not listening, and so I quit explaining and fell back a little farther from his pace. Jimmy Barrett was pounding on Clyde's chest when I walked up to within a few yards of where they were. The police chief had thrown his hat on the ground and was making a scratching, rubbing motion around his head. "You better get your father," he said. "I think this man is dead."

I looked at the blue face of Clyde and said to the police chief, "Are you going to cover him up?"

He turned to me and repeatedly harshly, "Get your father!"

My father was in his little office with the door locked. I pounded on the door and shouted, "It's an emergency."

My father came out on the porch and said, "Who is it?"

"It's Clyde, he's blue and he's not breathing, and he looks like he's had a heart attack."

"Clyde the wino?"

"I guess so." I didn't like to call Clyde a wino if he was dead.

"Well, is it Clyde the wino?"

"Yes."

My father turned and went back into the office. I heard him talking to one of his patients in an aggravated voice. He came back out on the porch, followed by a disheveled Gloria Strong. "I'll see you at the diner," he said.

We walked up Hill Avenue to the dealership. My father asked me a few questions about what had happened. I told him everything about the morning that I thought important. He walked quickly but not changing what I thought was a professional stride.

He was carrying his black bag in one hand and rubbing the face of his pocket watch with the thumb of the other. "It's unusual for a wino to die of a heart attack. How old was he?"

"I don't know. He was an army man."

"He was?"

"Yes, he got a check every month from the Army."

"Hmmmnn."

My father only spent a minute with Clyde. He raised himself up from the body and told Jimmy Barrett to collect Clyde's personal belongings and to call Windfield Waycross. "Tell Windfield that he was an army man," he said.

My father watched Gloria Strong walking up the street and absentmindedly rubbed the face of his pocket watch with his thumb.

"Will he get a military funeral?" I asked.

"If he requested one," my father said.

I turned to Mitch, who had been standing nearby, and said, "a soldier funeral."

Mitch shook his head up and down.

The screaming sound of the ambulance from the Waycross Funeral Home split the morning air. My father sighed a deep sigh and said, "That son of a bitch knows he's dead."

There were several people gathered around watching Windfield Waycross load the body into the ambulance. I heard a scuffle behind me and saw that Mitch was wrestling with Jimmy Barrett to keep him out of the little shed where he and Clyde had lived. I ran to Mitch and got him by the hand and led him aside. He stood and cried as Jimmy Barrett dragged blankets and pillows and a variety of collected items from the little shed. I walked over to where the police chief was and said, "I think all of the important stuff is in the brown army bag. He didn't care about the other stuff."

Jimmy Barrett looked through the bag for a minute and kicked his foot around among the other things and said, "That man will be responsible for this other stuff here." He was writing in a little notebook as he nodded toward Mitch.

After the ambulance had gone, Mitch came over to where I stood and handed me a cloth bag that looked like a woman's small purse. It had a note scrawled on the front of it which read:

> For James Friend,
> To be opened at my death.
>   Clyde Anderson

I never knew his name was Anderson.

I opened the small bag and looked inside to see a lot of money. There were bunches of twenty-dollar bills stacked neatly. I took the money from the bag and showed it to Mitch. He took the money from me and stared at it for a moment and then looked at me in a curious way. He took several of the bills from the pile and handed me the rest. He said nothing. I looked at the remaining money in awe. It seemed strange to be rewarded for someone's death. There was a note stuck between the bills. It read:

> James,
> Get the knife.
> Clyde.

Mitch moved all of Clyde's bedclothes and things to his side of the shed. He walked a lot that afternoon. His monologue was almost a whisper. I could not determine what he was saying as he ambled around the parking area. He finally sat down and started to rub his legs again. I was afraid. He would stop rubbing his legs, hold his breath and then suddenly gasp and continue to mumble. I went to the liquor store and bought a bottle of vodka and some cans of chicken and dumplings. We

didn't eat the dumplings, but we sipped on the vodka and I told Mitch stories of the many nice things that Clyde had done. I must have talked less than ten minutes before running out of things to say about Clyde. I realized that we had never done much and seldom talked. The silent part of our friendship could not be put into words, and I couldn't keep back the tears. When Mitch realized that I, too, was crying, he moved off to his shed and crawled inside. I didn't sleep that night. I might have dozed once or twice, but when the morning light came over the dealership I found the note Clyde had left me and read it again:

> James,
> Get the knife.
> Clyde.

I checked on Mitch and he was sleeping. I put twenty dollars in his shirt pocket. I thought of the beautiful four-bladed knife with the gold star embedded in the dark-brown wooden handle which I had tried to win from the crane machine at the carnival. I put the rest of the money back into the bag and walked to the Woodmont Coves Courthouse on McArthur Lane.

Mayor Arthur Lovette's receptionist was sitting at her desk and staring out the window when I walked into the mayor's outer office. She heard my footsteps and asked, "May I help you?"

"Yes. I want to know where the carnival went when it left here."

"The carnival?"

"Yes."

"You want to know where the carnival left for when it left Woodmont Coves and the Strawberry Festival?"

I looked at her. She started looking through some papers on her desk and said, "Maybe I know."

She came from behind her desk with a yellow envelope from which she took a yellow sheet of paper with a list of towns and dates on it. "Right now," she said, "they should be in Ingot, Indiana."

I asked if I could look at it, explaining that I was not sure I knew the spelling of "Ingot." She told me that I couldn't take the sheet with me.

She went back behind her desk and sat looking at me thoughtfully. "Do you have a complaint about them?" she asked.

"No."

I stood there holding the brown bag full of money. "Do you want any money?" I asked.

"There's no charge for information here, unless you want copies of something. The mayor is always glad to help any way he can." She was a pretty dark-haired girl with a different but appealing kind of body.

"I didn't want to pay you," I said. "I just wondered if you wanted any money."

I turned and went downstairs and out into the street. Jimmy Barrett stood by his police cruiser working on a small radio which he kept strapped to his belt.

He saw me and said, "You know, that guy who died over there this morning was a colonel in the Army at one time."

"I knew he was a colonel," I said. I knew no such thing.

I went to my trailer, got my salve bag, put some clothes in it, and walked to the bus station. There were only five or six people in the place that afternoon. I bought a thick book called *Get A Laugh Every Time*. It was a book of jokes to tell at parties and before making speeches. I bought a ticket to Ingot, Indiana, and was told that the bus would not leave until four in the afternoon. I sat down on a bench and started to read the book:

> I was in a bar one day and a man was in there with a dog with no legs. I said, "What's that dog's name?" Fella said, "It ain't got no name. It couldn't come if I called it anyway."

I started laughing as hard as I have ever laughed in my life. My sides began to hurt after a minute or two, and I started laughing out loud and walking around the bus station. I walked over to the man who had sold me the book and told him what I thought to be the funniest joke I had ever heard. Tears were streaming down my cheeks as I told the joke!

"I was in a bar one day and there was this guy with me called Clyde. A man asked me what his name was, and I said it wouldn't do any good to know. He can't come because he doesn't have a heart."

I started crying then. I couldn't help it. I walked away from the stunned man who had sold me the book and went to the rest room. I sat there crying until my eyes hurt. At four in the afternoon I caught the bus to Ingot, Indiana.

The seats on the bus were made of some velvetlike material. There was a lever on the side to move the back of the seat to a reclining position. I was halfway reclined and riding comfortably when I began to notice the odor. There was a smell of fuel in the bus. As I dwelled on it more and more, the odor became almost unbearable. I walked in a swaying manner to the front of the bus and asked the driver when we would arrive in Ingot. He ran his finger down a plastic-covered schedule above the windshield and said, "Two-thirty in the morning." We had been riding for about two hours, and I knew I could not stay aboard until the early hours of the morning. The bus pulled into what appeared to be a small town, or the outskirts of a big one. I was first off the bus with my salve bag and started walking away from the area of the bus station as quickly as possible. It was the same feeling of relief that I had experienced when I escaped from jail. I breathed the fresh afternoon air and walked toward a wooded area behind the bus station. There was a metal fence in my way, so I walked down the length of it until I found a place where dogs had been passing under. I crawled through the opening and went to sit behind a tree at the edge of a small ravine. I counted the money and learned that I had $650, not including what Mitch had taken. I tried to think of some great adventure I could have with the money. I tried to think of exotic things I could buy or do, but none came to mind.

I wondered if I would get the knife. I heard the

speaker system at the bus station call for passengers boarding the bus to Ingot, and I sat silently, looking over my shoulder to see if there was a commotion because of my absence. There was none, and the bus departed on time. It dawned on me that I was the only person in the world who knew who or where I was at that moment. I looked around at the strange place I had landed and was pleased.

 The Laughing Man walked steadily and grimly, toward the huge fire that he had going in the field behind his house. He carried his scrapbook with him now. It was filled with pictures of his performances and of him with celebrities and dignitaries. It was a large black bulky book. He held it almost fondly for a moment and then flung it toward the fire. The book did not sail as he had thought it would. The pages caught the air and the book flopped like a wounded bird and fell short of the flames. The Laughing Man rushed toward the book, picked it up, and placed it neatly on top of the flames, singeing the hair on his arms.

He made trip after trip from his house to the fire in the field. In the heat of the fire on this warm day a perspiring, struggling, fat, and flushed madman was trying frantically to destroy his past.

There were wooden speaker cabinets, plaid suits, posters, letters, records, and all manner of show business memorabilia glowing in the fire. Some of it burned, but some of it smouldered and fought against destruction.

The fire burned slowly and tortuously. The Laughing Man found a long pole and began to poke the fire and stir it to efficiency. He worried the burning mass of rubble far into the evening, and he could be seen late that night digging a hole to bury the stubborn remains.

The rest of the night was spent walking through the house and looking for any trace of his past. Every article he touched or saw reminded him of who he was and what he did. He carried a bottle of scotch in his hand and swung it wildly about him as he searched for reminders of the past. In drunken frustration he finally started a fire on the living-room floor and went to a vantage point down the long drive to watch the beautiful house burn high into the evening sky. He sat there, drunk and shocked, long after the fire trucks and curiosity seekers had gone. All that remained of his house were smouldering ashes. A blue van approached The Laughing Man, circled the drive and tossed a newspaper at him. As the van disappeared down the road, he read the bold headline:

LAUGHING MAN'S HOUSE BURNS

Sitting behind the bus station in God Knows Where, I missed Claudia Barnes. I wish I had gotten to know her better. She was the person I feared most. I was afraid of Joe Morgan, but I knew enough about him to cope. Claudia Barnes, on the other hand, was a mystery and possessed genius of some kind to have managed such an extraordinary life with such confidence and control. I hit myself in the head trying to find something that would give me a way of thinking as she had thought. I admired her. I pictured myself with three wives:

"I'm going to take my bath now. Anybody wants to come here and get some of me after I've had my bath, I'll be here and waiting and smelling like a rose. You get out of line and start playing with yourself I'll know about it, and I'll whip you bad. Get everything in order, and keep this place running smooth or there'll be no more wine and no more untellable tales for any of you."

My God, how did all of that work, and why, and whose idea was it in the first place? It was stunning to think about. It made me realize how much of a difference there is in people and how dangerous it is to know so much and not understand.

It was Claudia Barnes I missed. I was picking the worst and pretending a generosity of nostalgia in order to include the rest of the town. I was homesick already.

I walked back to the bus station. I could have gone in any direction, but I felt an obligation to go back and make some kind of apology for not continuing the trip with them.

At the bus station I asked a taxi driver to take me to a motel. I had never spent a night in a motel, and I asked the driver if I should have made any previous arrangement. The driver sighed and said, "No, you'll get in all right, I imagine."

I paid in advance and was told that if I made any phone calls or charged anything to my room I would have to stop and pay for it before I checked out.

I slept well in the soft bed and on the clean sheets in this small home away from home. There was only a Bible to read.

There was a girl outside my window by the pool the next morning. I took the money from the bag and counted it again and watched the girl by the pool. The money was too much to look at, and the girl was too pretty to look at. I stood in the shower for a long time and thought about the money and the girl. I knew that Clyde had intended for me to make more use of the money than just buying the knife. There was so much money.

I dressed in clean jeans and a shirt and went out to look at the swimming pool and the girl. I sat in a plastic chair with my salve bag and my money close at hand. The girl seemed to have a lot of things with her: There was the lotion she rubbed on her knees from time to time; she had a book she read now and then; she had a towel; a pair of sunglasses; a small bag that she dug into on occasion; and a wide yellow hat that contrasted with her small black one-piece bathing suit. Her blond hair shone in the sun, and her body seemed to be so well proportioned that it defied description. Although I was the only other person at the pool, she had not noticed me—or pretended she hadn't. I was convinced she was not aware of me, so I walked around the pool as if I were looking for fish. I heard a voice say, "It's not that deep."

I turned and looked at her lying partially reclined on the plastic lounge chair and thought I could see blond, sun-bleached pubic hair protruding from the bottom of her black bathing suit. I had never been in love before and had no idea what to say or what to do.

I said, "In the marines they teach you to watch water pretty close. How deep it is can fool you sometimes."

There was no reply. I said, "Water is both a lifesaver and a life-taker. It can be a friend or an enemy. I didn't want you to go jumping in here and getting yourself hurt or scared unless it was all right."

I was standing looking into the water as I made that speech, afraid to look at her. She said, "Do you like cantaloupe? My father is a wholesale produce distributor for this area. I get to come here a week early to line up a few customers. My father says it isn't necessary, but I get to get away from my brothers and sisters for a whole week. My mother used to do this job, but she died a few years ago. And now, since I'm the oldest, I made my father let me do it. I like to travel and do and see things."

I stood there by the pool, surprised by the long speech, and said, "I sure like cantaloupe." I turned to see her sitting on the edge of the seat lighting a cigarette.

She said, "Do you drink?"

I said, "No, no. The one thing my folks taught me was never to drink. I think it makes a fool out of a person. I'm not drinking. I've just had a lot happen to me in the last few days."

"Well, they have a nice lounge in this place, but I hate to go in by myself and I thought maybe we could go in and get a drink. Do you know what a piña colada is?"

"No, not really, but I think it's all right if a person has a drink now and then. My father is a doctor, and he says it's relaxing."

She started gathering up her things and said, "I'll meet you in the lounge in a few minutes. I can't very well wear this in there." She patted herself on her flat stomach, indicating the one-piece bathing suit, and laughed an open little laugh that I wish I could imitate.

I said, "Okay. I'll meet you in the lounge as soon as you get there."

I went back to my room, took some of the twenties from the salve bag and hid the bag under the bed. I closed the drapes and walked around the motel into the lobby and saw the little red neon light that read "Lounge."

 Maude Primm sat sipping from a bowl of chicken noodle soup and listening to the rain. It had been raining for fourteen or fifteen hours, and the occasional flash of lightning had awakened her from a restless sleep. She sat at a small wooden table and stared at the freezer that contained the body of Dr. Friedman. She was tired of the vigil the freezer imposed upon her. What could she be waiting for? There would never be a

way to bring anyone back to life, and she knew well that she didn't want Dr. Friedman back anyway.

She was startled out of her drowsiness by a banging on the door. She yelled, "Wait a minute," picked her robe off the bed, placed it around her shoulders, and opened the apartment door.

Jimmy Barrett stood there in a monstrous-looking yellow raincoat and hat and practically screamed at her. "Maude, you're gonna have to get out of this apartment, the Boo River is flooding, and it looks like it's gonna get out of its banks and be in the whole town in a little while. The water is already ankle deep out here on Main Street. Bo and Lydia's store is about flooded out."

"Don't yell, Jimmy, I'm not deaf and I can swim. Water's not going to get this high."

"That don't make no difference. You won't be able to get out of here in a little bit. It's coming up fast."

Maude put her hand against the apartment door and closed it as she said, "Okay, okay. I'll get out as soon as I can."

The Boo River flooded every year about the same time and Maude knew that it would not—could not—get to a second-story apartment. The pharmacy downstairs was no longer her responsibility, so she started to sit down and finish her soup.

Maude went to the window and saw the water, sticks, mud, and debris rushing along the gutters of Main Street. "It'll clean this damned old town out," she thought.

Maude went to the phone and dialed the Waycross

Funeral Home. Windfield Waycross answered in an excited voice that made Maude think he was hoping someone would drown in all of the water. "Hello, Windfield here."

"Windfield, this is Maude Primm. You're on high ground up there. How high is this water going to get?"

"It looks to me like it's gonna be the worst one we've ever had, Maude. I saw a doghouse go down the river a few minutes ago. There's *everything* in that river and folks are gonna get hurt, you can count on that. Oh, are you okay?"

"Yes, I'm fine, Windfield. Jimmy Barrett came by here hollering and shouting like he was loading an ark. Call me if it gets to lookin' worse."

"Are you in your apartment?"

"Yes, I'm high and dry."

"Well, you better have everything you need up there 'cause it's gonna get worse."

"Okay, call me if you think so."

Maude hung up the phone and thought again about how the water would clean out the town. She walked to the freezer and lifted the lid and looked down at Dr. Friedman, who was turning a chalky, icy white. She reached in to take hold of his arm to move his body. It would not move. She bent farther over into the freezer and started pulling on his legs and then his head. The body would not budge. Maude stood back from the freezer with a look of disgust.

Walking over to the sink, she picked up a small pan and started running hot water into it. She could not resist the thought that Dr. Friedman had spent a lot of time in hot water lately. Maude shrugged off the silly thought and walked to the freezer and poured in the water. There was a hissing sound as the hot water hit the ice in the freezer. After several pans of water and much pulling and jerking, she had the body out in the center of the floor, lying on its side in a sitting position. She sat the body up on its buttocks and began trying to bend it back into a prone position. The body would not bend.

Maude went to the cupboard and selected her heaviest knife. She bent over the frozen body and laid it on its back with the feet against the freezer. She started chopping at the fingers. They were easier to break than they were to cut, so she settled for laying the edge of the knife along the hand just below the knuckles and hitting the back of the blade with her shoe. The fingers broke away from the hand, and she used the same procedure for the thumbs. Placing the fingers and thumbs in the pocket of her coat, she plugged in the iron and sat perspiring as she waited for it to heat. When the iron was hot, she managed to get it far enough up under the hands to sear the palms. The odor of the burning flesh caused her to retch. She staggered, vomiting, toward the door. There were small pieces of flesh on the iron. She flung it down the stairwell and stood gasping as the iron sizzled in the water now gathering at the bottom of the stairs. There would be no fingerprints or palm prints if the body was ever found.

Maude Primm went to her bed and started taking off the sheets. She wrapped the body in the sheets and used the cord from the drapes to tie them around the neck, torso and feet. It was a small, wet, icy package that Maude Primm carried from her apartment that morning. She threw the body on the front seat of her car and drove east on Hill Avenue, turned right on Hill Road, and drove to the bridge crossing the raging Boo River. She was on high ground now and could see the traffic from both directions. She waited until the road was clear and then dropped her package into the river. The body, wrapped in white sheets, rose and fell with the water as if it were dancing out of sight.

Maude sat in her car for a few minutes as the rain beat against the windshield. She leaned her head on the steering wheel and began to cry, for Dr. Friedman was finally gone—or so she thought.

The lounge was dimly lit as I walked in and found a seat in a back corner of the odd-shaped room. There were barstools to the left of the door around a long bar with hundreds of different-colored bottles stacked here and there. Glass shelves held sparkling glasses of different shapes. The heavy red-haired lady who was the bartender leaned on one elbow and talked to the only customer in the place. A thin young man in a red shirt was sweeping a small dance floor. I sat and stared at the small red flame floating in a red glass on my table.

It was a short wait for the pretty girl. She came bouncing through the door wearing a yellow dress and brown slippers, swinging a brown handbag. The dress was the same shade of yellow as the hat she had had with her at the pool. I thought the hat would have gone well with her attire. She waved at the people in the lounge and called each of them by name. She had obviously been in the place before. She ordered a drink on her way to the table, sat down and asked, "What'll you have?"

"Do they have sloe gin?"

The heavy red-haired lady said, "You want it up or on the rocks?"

I said, "What?"

The young blond lady said, "You want it with or without ice?"

"No ice," I said.

The girl put her hand on my shoulder and looked at me and said, "I don't even know your name. I'm Brenda."

"I'm James."

"Do they call you Jim?"

"No, James."

"Well, it makes you sound like a chauffeur or something." With that she tossed her head and laughed a loud laugh that almost filled the lounge. It was startling and yet open and inoffensive. Her legs were bare and her time by the pool had been well spent. Her bra was a light tan and when she moved—which she did a lot—you could tell where her tan left off and her natural skin color started. She caught me looking at her cleavage and poked my chest with her finger.

I managed a small laugh and felt better.

I paid for the drinks and we went unsteadily to my room and sat on the edge of the bed for a few minutes. She smoked a cigarette and told me more stories about her family. She jumped from the bed and asked why I didn't have any luggage. I told her it was under the bed, and she announced that she was going to get into something comfortable. I could hear the shower running in the bathroom as I finished off the sloe gin I had brought from the lounge. She came out of the bathroom wrapped in a white towel that stretched from her knees to her breasts. I knew I had never seen any woman as beautiful in all my life. She came over to the bed and sat and then lay back on the orange spread and took a deep sigh. I lay down on the bed beside her and removed the towel from her body and spread it out on either side of her. She lay quiet and beautiful as I kissed her. She passed her hand through my hair and didn't change positions. As the sloe gin eased through my veins, I put my head on the pillow beside her and was as happy as I have ever been.

It was dark in the room when I awoke. I didn't know where I was for a moment. I tried to look around the room for something familiar. I reached for the girl. She was not there. I found the light and turned it on. There was a towel lying on the bed beside me. I rushed into the bathroom. I ran to the window and opened the drapes. It was dark outside, and the only light was the light from the corner of the building that illuminated the walkways for the customers of the motel. The pool area was dark.

I remembered my salve bag and reached under the bed for it. The bag was there, and the money was in the little brown zipper bag inside. I sat on the edge of the bed, disgusted and saddened. I realized I did not feel well.

There were several people in the lounge when I went by there, but Brenda was not one of them. I asked the lady at the desk how far it was to Ingot, Indiana. She shook her head and said, "I've never heard of it."

I went back to the lounge and asked the heavy red-haired lady if she had seen Brenda. She threw a tray of beer bottles into a trash can and said, "Her husband picked her up about eight. They live around here some-where. She just comes over to use the pool."

 Lydia Strong was tired and haggard-looking. The mud had been four inches deep in Strong's Supermarket, and she resented knowing that only water can wash away what water has brought. She hosed down the aisles of the store one more time, knowing that each time more silt and mud would creep out from under the stock shelves that would have to be mopped and swept away. Through the glass doors of the market she had yelled all day, "We are closed until tomorrow." Bo Strong had stayed until the water had made it impossible to stack any more of the groceries on higher shelves. He had done well, and they had not lost much stock. There were some feed and grain bags in the back that had gotten wet, but Bo could offer those to hog and cattle people for a bargain price; they would be gone in a few days, replaced by the sweet, dry sacks of new stock.

Bo Strong looked at the bare parking lot of the

supermarket. He would have to buy a few loads of gravel to cover it again. He really didn't mind the flood in a way. He had been meaning to re-gravel the drive and haul away a lot of the old boxes and debris that had gathered behind his market. Now the flood had done all of that work for him, and he felt a small sense of relief. It was woman's work to clean the mud from the store, so he stayed out back to take care of the heavy work—work that the flood had already done.

Bo Strong walked slower and slower as he approached the white something hanging on the iron bar that was hooked on the edge of the loading ramp behind his store. The closer he got and the more he thought he'd say, the slower he moved. He was within six feet of the object when he yelled for his wife. "Lydia, Ly-di-aaaaaa!"

Dr. John Friend, who served as coroner, looked at the wet package lying in the Waycross Funeral Home preparation room and said, "Well gentlemen, it looks like Dr. Friedman to me, too. But with no fingers and the palms of the hands the way they are, I'm for calling it an unknown body."

Jimmy Barrett stomped around the room and scratched his head. "Doc, I'd bet next month's pay that this is the old doc."

"I don't care how much this body reminds us of Dr. Friedman. We can't say this is Dr. Friedman just because we knew him. The graveyard is at the other end of town, and this body obviously came downriver! The cemetery has not been flooded. What I'm telling you, Windfield, is that we had better leave this damned mess alone. There are no dental records, this man has been buried without his teeth, and has been in a room like this before because his lips are sewn together from the inside in preparation for burial."

Windfield Waycross said, "I agree. This is not Dr. Friedman because I buried his teeth, as requested. I suggest we turn this matter over to the state police or the sheriff and pretend not to know anything about it. It just stirs up speculation."

Dr. Friend sat on the edge of the preparation table and shook his head. "If I know anything about being dead, I would think old Doc Friedman would be a pile of dust by now. I have never in my life seen anything that beats this."

He rubbed his thumb on his pocket watch and gave Windfield Waycross his instructions. "Report an unknown body washed ashore at Woodmont Coves. Keep Lydia out of it; she didn't find the body. Bo is as upset about this as anybody; he won't want to get involved."

Windfield Waycross came along behind John Friend as he left the funeral home. He tugged at Dr. Friend's coat and asked, "Do you think we ought to put him back in the same place they got him?"

John Friend turned in anger and shouted, "Dammit, Windfield, we don't know whose body this is. If they give you an order to bury him, just bury him."

Bo Strong said that he didn't know anything except that he saw the package and called the police. Jimmy Barrett said he couldn't make any identification without teeth, and the body had no fingers for fingerprints. Windfield Waycross was given orders to bury the body.

Windfield Waycross stood above the grave and looked down at the brown wooden box. "You'd have been better off to stay wherever you were, Doctor."

I asked the heavy red-haired lady if she knew how I could get to the highway leading to Ingot, Indiana. A truck driver in the bar answered my question by saying he was headed that way in a few minutes and would give me a ride.

I sat high above the road and nursed my salve bag in my lap as the driver bumped and rattled his way to Ingot. He pulled over to the side of the road after about two hours and said, "Thar she blows, kid!" I looked out the high window and saw the lights of a town some distance away. "Slow me down if I get in there; ain't much of a walk, though."

I thanked him for the ride and jumped to the ground. I started walking toward the lights and encountered a high fence between me and the open field before the town. I had a good deal of trouble getting over the fence, as it had some kind of barbed wire across the top. I made my way across the field and stood in front of a café. I entered and sat at the counter. The waitress brought me a cup of coffee. I said, "I don't drink coffee."

She hit her fist against the counter and said, "What do you want?"

"I'll have a hamburger with everything and a Coke."

"The coffee is on the house," she said.

I sipped the coffee. It tasted bitter and was hot. I waited for the hamburger and Coke. When they were brought, I asked the waitress if there was a carnival in town. She waved her hand toward the back of the restaurant. "There's a carnival over there as big as all get-out. They'll be in here after a while if you don't want to look for 'em."

I walked around behind the restaurant and saw the lights of the carnival in the field below. There was a narrow road that ran along the edge of the hill and down toward the valley. It was not the main road, but it was a better way to walk than to go back out in front of the restaurant and walk all the way around the valley. I went down the narrow road toward the lights and the noise.

Although there were some different rides and games at this site, it would have convinced almost anybody that the show was still in Woodmont Coves. There was a stand just to the left of the entrance gate where a man was guessing weights. He had rows and rows of Indian blankets all around him. He was shouting his spiel as I approached him. "Guess your weight here. If I miss it by a pound you can sleep upon the ground. Win a beautiful one hundred percent Indian blanket if I can't tell your weight within a pound."

I interrupted his sales pitch and asked him if he would sell one of the blankets. He motioned me to step on the scales. "Step right up here, son, and win one of these blankets. It's only fifty cents for the guess, and you might well win one of these collector's items."

"I want to buy one," I explained.

"Why, do you know what one of these blankets would cost a man if he bought one? Why, it'd cost nearly twenty dollars to buy one of these blankets. Step right up here and let me take a guess."

"I'll give you twenty dollars." I stood and stared at the man for a minute before he spoke.

"Now, look, I didn't say you *could* buy one of these blankets for twenty dollars. What I said was, if you could buy one it would cost that much and probably a lot more. Why, son, these blankets came from a real reservation in Oklahoma. Why, these things are priceless—almost."

I stared at him until he handed one of the blankets to me. I gave him the twenty dollars and walked away. He called after me, "Hey, Boy, that'll be two dollars tax on that blanket. We're running a real business here, not some game."

I kept walking until I was out of hearing range. I turned away from the midway of the carnival and walked around behind the tents out into an open field. There were some old cars sitting along the edge of the field that had been abandoned. I crawled into the back-seat of one of the cars, wrapped myself in the Indian blanket and fell fast asleep.

I woke up the next morning with a stiff neck. I could hardly get out of the car. It hurt me to move. I crawled down to the floor of the car and managed to roll out onto the ground. It was one of the most painful things I had ever experienced. I had to turn my whole body in order to look in different directions. I rubbed the back of my neck until it was red. I finally sat still against the side of the car until the pain was bearable. I stuffed my Indian blanket part way into my salve sack and walked across the field to the carnival grounds.

There were people, mostly carnival workers, moving all around the grounds. I passed up several offers to earn a quarter or fifty cents on my way in search of The Hamburger Girl. I found her cooking hamburgers and sausage sandwiches for her fellow workers. She recognized me when I ordered a hamburger. She rolled back on her heels and punched a sandy-haired, blue-jeaned young lady at the counter and said, "Hey, Sheila, di is da boay I tole you stole my dress." She laughed and rubbed me on the head. "How you been, boay, and wat chu doin way up here?"

"I want you to do something for me."

"You give me a name fo it, and I'll see you got it rite off."

I looked at the sandy-haired girl. She shrugged her shoulders, slipped off the stool and walked away. The Hamburger Girl looked after her and said, "Dat gal can dance a pecker up fastern I can cook a burger, you can count on it."

I explained to her that I wanted her to buy the knife from the crane game. She didn't understand at first. I described the game and the knife in detail until she knew what I meant. I had to impress upon her how important it was to me. She said, "I caint leave heah rite now, but you go tell dat man in dat striped tent dat I woan see him rite dis minute."

"What's his name?"

"Jelly Balls, just call him Jelly Balls."

I walked down to the tent and found a huge man sorting out little toys of one kind or another. He had the trinkets spread around on the ground and was placing them in small brown bags. I said, "Uh, Mr. Jelly . . ."

His head jerked up, and he glared at me and shouted, "Who in hell you calling Jelly, boy?"

I quickly explained that the lady at the hamburger stand wanted to see him. He calmed down a little and walked around the front of the tent and yelled at The Hamburger Girl, "What is it?"

The Hamburger Girl motioned for him to come to her. The big man lumbered up toward the hamburger stand with me right behind him. When we were in speaking range The Hamburger Girl said, "I want you to give dis boay dat come on knife in dat joke machine you operating."

The huge man looked at me and groaned, "Ah, come on, I'm doing all right with that knife. Some joker in a few towns back got one of them things some- way. What's this kid need with it?"

The Hamburger Girl slapped her hand against the counter with a loud bang. "You wanna starve yo ass off on de road all summer? I said go git dat knife."

The huge man looked at me as if I were some sort of informer. He ambled off down the midway and came back in a few minutes and handed me the knife. I held the knife in my hand and stared at it. The huge man whispered to me, "I hope you cut your pecker off, you asshole."

"Lay offen him," The Hamburger Girl yelled.

He went back to his tent to sort his tiny toys.

The Hamburger Girl looked at me in a quizzical way. "You come roun heah tonite and tell me wat you been up to, and I'll hug yo neck. I'm rite busy rite now."

I thanked her and went back to the car I had slept in the night before. The knife was not as big as I remembered it being. Maybe that was one of the tricks of the crane machine. It was probably a trick of the mind. Always, when I had at last gotten a dream in hand, it had not seemed as pretty or as satisfying as it had first appeared. I wondered if Clyde would be proud of me.

 The Laughing Man drove his big, expensive car round and round the town. He liked the motion of the car and the power of it. He was bored but frightened. The motel he had been staying in had grown tiresome and small. His feeling of freedom from the past had dulled somewhat, and now he was looking for some way to use his energies. He drove up Route 52 toward Woodmont Coves. He liked the idea of the hills. The hills seemed a good place to be near a good thought, and a good place to contemplate his future. He drove until he was well within the hill country. Then he turned his car to the side of the road, got out, and walked through a clump of bushes out into the woods at the side of the road. When he was well out of sight of the road, he took off his jacket, his shoes, his shirt, his trousers and, in fact, all of his clothes.

It was a strange sight. He laid all of his clothes out into a sort of bed and lay down on them and stared into the leaves of the oak just above him. He was not surprised to see The Thinking Man standing there in front of him. The Thinking Man was dressed in absolute white. Shoes, socks, suit, tie—everything about The Thinking Man's costume was white, including his hair.

The Laughing Man sat upright and addressed the white-suited gentleman. "And now what am I to think?"

The Thinking Man, a man of good humor and gracious disposition, smiled a pleasant smile and said, "How would you like to think, high or small?"

"What is the difference, as you see it, in thinking high or small?" said The Laughing Man.

The Thinking Man made his speech:

"Man is tribal. You have a choice of tribes. Some you can join and others you cannot. If you choose to think small, you must accept the ways of small thinking. You must learn to bowl, play golf, play bridge . . . Such games are games within the game. *The* game of life. If you choose to think high, you might become a man of the universe. You must question the order of things. The word you must learn to understand is "why." Why is God in charge, and who is He? Why life? Why this contest between good and evil, and whose game is it? Why are you mostly round and not square? Who stands to win or lose by your activities and your thoughts? Why do you seem to be a pawn in the universal game of existence? Remember that you are tribal. You must join one club or another. Some clubs you cannot join. The Church is the only high-thinking group that you can subscribe to at the moment. The Church has one problem, however; it lays claim to high thinking and asks the big question, but it provides you with small-thinking answers. There are those in the Church who do high thinking . . . and when they get to know you they will share the high questions with you. There are many tribes among you. Join one, or you will die without the answer, never having asked the question. I must go now. I have a lot of thinking to do with my tribe."

The Laughing Man thanked the now invisible Thinking Man and donned his clothes and was off to find a pretty church; pretty churches have money, he thought.

I crawled over the fence and put my thumb out and caught a ride back along the same route I had come. There were no people going direct, but I caught enough rides to bring me back to where I wanted to be—the motel in the town where I had stopped on the way to Ingot.

The heavy red-haired woman was still at the bar. When I arrived late in the evening, I looked around the odd-shaped bar until I was sure Brenda was not there. I bought some crackers and candy from machines in the hallway and slept in my room until the sun shone through my window.

When I woke up I went quickly to the window and

looked out at the pool area. There was a man in a red bathing suit jumping in and out of the pool. He would occasionally look around to see if anyone was watching, then puff out his chest and dive headlong into the pool and take exaggerated strokes until he reached the other side. I watched him in disgust.

I took my clean shirt and jeans out of the salve bag and then showered long and diligently. I put most of the money into the salve bag under the mattress. There were bags under my eyes and red spots on my cheeks. I bought some shaving lotion and a toothbrush from one of the vending machines. I went to the coffee shop and ordered a hamburger with everything and a Coke. There was a newspaper article that told of a body that had washed up on the shores of Woodmont Coves during the recent flooding. Police believed it to be the body of a young teenager. I puzzled over the story for a minute or two. My father's house was in the low part of town, but the article mentioned no casualties, so I went about eating my breakfast. I lingered over my food until I saw her coming up the sidewalk three blocks away. There was no mistake about the walk and the yellow dress. She turned into the far side of the motel toward the pool before she reached the area where I was sitting.

I walked into the lounge, which the red-haired heavy woman was just opening. She did not remember seeing me before. I ordered two piña coladas.

I walked straight toward Brenda, who was sitting in one of the plastic chairs in her black one-piece bathing suit. I wondered what she had done with the yellow hat. She didn't look up when she saw me coming. I walked around behind her chair, holding the two piña coladas in my hands. I reached around in front of her and touched her nose with one of the drinks. She never missed a beat as she lowered her book and took the white, cold glass from my hand. "Good morning, James," she said.

"Do you like cantaloupe?" I said.

She laughed the loud laugh again. "Nothing I like better," she said.

I walked around in front of her and said, "I had to see you again. I'm sorry about the other night. I must have been exhausted."

She tossed her head and smiled at me. "Oh, you were not that tired. When I left the room you looked as if you had a carrot in your pants." She laughed the small laugh now.

"Isn't this a beautiful spot for this time of year?" I said. "It seems nature picks a certain spot in the country and blesses it with a special time of the year. There's Florida in the winter, Colorado in the winter, Europe in the spring . . . life is a wonderful experience if one can travel."

Brenda looked at me with mild surprise and said, "Why, that sounds almost poetic. I love poetry." She finished her drink in one long swallow; I handed her the other one and took the empty glass from her hand. She smiled at me with her beautiful white teeth and said, "Are you trying to ply me with drinks?"

I said, "No, I'm catering to your every wish. You are the most fascinating woman I have ever met."

She finished off the second drink in a few quick swallows and said, "Do you still have a room here?"

I said, "I certainly do."

She looked around the pool area and said, "Get me a couple more piña coladas and I'll meet you there. What room is it?"

I said, "Room two twenty-eight."

"Five minutes," she said.

The routine was almost the same as before. She finished her drinks, told stories of her fictitious family and smoked cigarettes before taking her shower. She came from the bathroom wearing the towel and a smile. She lay back on the bed beside me as before. I took the towel from around her and spread it on both sides. She lay with her pink nipples pointed toward the star-spangled ceiling of the motel. I made love to her while she made funny noises with her throat and her breath. She lay silently beside me and said, "Could we do it again later?"

I said, "My pleasure."

I reached under the bed for the pretty four-bladed knife with the gold star embedded in the handle. I noiselessly opened the largest blade. I leaned toward her and placed the knife at her eye level. She did not see the knife at first glance. She scooted back toward the headboard of the bed and gasped as she saw the shiny metal of the blade. She fainted.

I folded the blade back into the knife, gathered my salve bag and quietly closed the door of the motel room. I walked across a field to the nearest main highway and put my thumb into the air . . . laughing, laughing, laughing.

Willie Alexander came into the Waycross Funeral Home flipping the white cloth that he had tied around his wrist. Colonel Clyde Anderson's body lay stretched in a gray casket with an American flag folded and lying at the bottom. Willie Alexander signed the guest book and took a seat in the rear of the chapel. Windfield Waycross was saying something and gesturing with his hands.

Windfield lifted his head toward Willie and said, "Did you know this man, Willie?"

"Yes, sir, we had mutual friends."

Windfield could not for the life of him figure out what Willie Alexander was talking about. Funeral chapels were public places, so he went about his work. A tired-looking old man had just brought some flowers to the door and was mumbling to himself about Clyde and James. Windfield was finding a nice way to display the two small wreaths that had been brought to the chapel. He placed one of his standard plastic wreaths in the middle and placed the two real ones on either side of the casket. Willie Alexander was standing looking down at the body of Clyde Anderson. He was saying something in what Windfield thought was a harsh tone.

Windfield Waycross went out the chapel door and picked up a broom to sweep out the back of his hearse.

Willie Alexander worked quickly. He reached into the casket, up under the backless suit worn by Clyde Anderson, moved his hand down over the gauze that covered the incision where the intestines had been removed from the body, found Clyde Anderson's penis, and severed it with one quick stroke of the razor. He folded the razor, placed the penis in his pocket, and smoothed the suit back around the side of the body. Windfield was picking up the flower and fern debris that he had swept from the hearse. Willie flipped the white cloth at Windfield as he stepped down the walk in front of the funeral home. He looked back at Windfield and said in a singsong voice, "I'll have a nice memory of my friend in there."

Windfield picked up a handful of the fern and flower debris and held it to his nose. He had always thought it had a wonderful smell.

Dodd Givens was leaning on the counter when Willie Alexander came into the hardware store. "Can I help?" Dodd said.

"Do you sell alcohol?" Willie asked.

"We got some quart bottles back there, but I think you'd want to get some from the drugstore if you want to use it for any kind of medical reasons."

"Just so it's alcohol," Willie said.

That night in his room Willie Alexander was startled to see the male organ start to expand and lengthen as it lay at the bottom of the jar of alcohol. It would be something he would have to show his friends. He stared at it as he masturbated.

I stopped at a service station to use the rest room and bought a little folded map in order to find my way back to Woodmont Coves. I got as far as Middletown, riding with an old junk dealer who had been on a collection trip, as he called it. "You'd be surprised what some folk'll throw away," he said. "This morning, up the road a piece, I got a horse collar almost a hundred years old—in good shape, too. See, what you do is you take this horse collar and rub a little shoe polish into some of the bare spots, and you get it looking shiny and clean and then you put a mirror inside of it, and some folk'll pay a lot of money for it and hang it in their house. You'd be surprised what some folk'll hang in their houses."

It was such an energetic speech, and such an explanatory one, that I felt guilty not really having a reply, so I said, "That's interesting."

The old man leaned back in his seat and took a long, deep breath, "If you're going to Woodmont Coves, I'm gonna have to let you off down here 'cause I got some business here in Middletown."

The truck rattled to the side of the street. I got my salve bag and jumped to the sidewalk. "Thanks for the ride."

I stood there looking around for a minute. I wanted to find the road to Woodmont Coves. It was a minute before I realized I was standing across the street from the police station. I put my head down and started walking as fast as I could. After a few minutes I realized that I was getting farther from the main part of town. I turned back toward what I thought was the business section and came down the street toward the bus station. There was a cab parked along the side of the building that housed the bus station. I walked over and awakened the driver, who was dozing in the driver's seat. He sat up quickly and seemed to be wide awake. "I'm free," he said.

"How much would it cost me to go to Woodmont Coves?"

He sat up a little straighter and looked at me suspiciously. "Woodmont Coves is twenty-six miles from here."

"I know."

"Well, it'll cost you eight dollars to get to Woodmont Coves."

"Okay."

"That'll be eight dollars before we leave."

I counted out the eight dollars, handed it to him and got into the backseat.

He said, "Wait a minute, sir," and went into the bus station to say something to one of the girls behind a ticket window.

We finally drove a few turns around Middletown until we hit Route 52 and the road to Woodmont Coves.

I had the cabdriver drop me off at the dealership on Hill Avenue. Mitch was sitting in his usual place but did not see me arrive. I was glad; it would have confused him to see me riding in a taxi. I sat down with my back against the wall of the dealership and fondled the knife in my hand. When Mitch noticed me and the knife, I handed it to him. He turned it over and over in his hands for a few minutes and then handed it to me, pointing to some small lettering on the back. The letters read "Made in Japan."

Mitch sat looking at my salve bag. I took out the

Indian blanket and handed it to him. He placed it around his shoulders and started to giggle. I was so startled by his giggling that I started to laugh, too. Mitch pulled the blanket up around his neck with both hands and said, "Well, hoo and hoo, and good morning, man." It was a gift.

I walked down Hill Avenue past my father's house and turned left on Fourth Street and walked up to the Waycross Funeral Home. Windfield Waycross sat at his desk with his feet up. He started to get up and then recognized me and waved me in. " 'lo, James."

"Hello, Mr. Waycross." I looked around the room and did not see a funeral in progress. "Has Mr. Cl——, uh, Mr. Anderson been buried?"

Windfield stood up from his desk and said, "Why, yes, he was buried yesterday afternoon. Anything you need?"

"No, I just wondered."

I walked over and handed him the knife. "Mr. Anderson gave me that. He left it for me in his will."

Windfield Waycross scratched his chin and said, "You know, James, Mr. Anderson was a fine man and a credit to his country. I wish I had gotten to know him better."

Windfield turned the knife over and over in his hand and held it up to the light. I could tell that he was reading the small print on the back.

 Dr. John Friend found out about Maude Primm's involvement in the reappearance of Dr. Friedman's body. He did not put much emphasis on the legal matters that came up in his activities as county coroner. He also did not trouble himself with the fine print in the advanced theories on ethics in medicine. There were many "sleeping dogs" in local medical histories, and he intended to let them lie. People who looked upon doctors as small gods had a right to, as he saw it. If one wanted to place one's body in the hands of a doctor for safekeeping, for surgery, for mental alteration by way of drugs, and sometimes unwitting research, that was the patient's business and the patient's responsibility. Few saw things as Dr. Friend did.

Maude Primm had acted coolly in the finding of the body, which was washed ashore at Strong's Supermarket. She refused to come and identify the remains in that loathsome package and said she saw no reason to be involved.

When the young lady from Woodmont Dry Cleaners called to say that she had found something awful in Maude Primm's coat pockets, Dr. Friend calmed the crying girl by telling her that he would come right over. At the dry cleaners Dr. Friend thought the fingers to be those of the man whose body had been washed ashore. They were of the right size and had been cut along the same knuckle as the missing fingers of the corpse. Dr. Friend quieted the crying girl by telling her that the fingers were not fingers but tissue samples that Maude was supposed to send away for analysis in Middletown. The package in which they were originally put must have broken open, and the tissue sample had simply fallen out into Maude's coat pocket. Dr. Friend retrieved all of the members and wrapped them in a handkerchief. He told the young lady to clean the coat and think no more of it. He thanked her for calling and left the dry cleaners as the young lady furiously washed her hands.

Back at his office, Dr. Friend placed the fingers in a small glass container filled with formaldehyde. He placed the bottle on a shelf above his desk and tried to piece together some line of reasoning for all this latest news.

Jimmy Barrett called to inquire about the fingers. John Friend said calmly, "Just some sample tissue that I was sending to Middletown, Jimmy. Just some sample tissue."

Jimmy Barrett was silent for a minute, then he said, "Oh, I see. Well, that girl was shook up." He paused again and added, "We could, uh, use some fingers around here, if you know what I mean?"

John Friend hung up the phone. He took his watch from his vest pocket and started rubbing the face of it with his thumb.

Jimmy Barrett pulled his police car into the little lane that led down to the Boo River. He got out of the car and placed his hands on the sides of his head and stretched and yawned. Jimmy walked around to the rear of the car and opened the trunk. There were several bottles of whiskey, gin, rum, and brandy lying among the police gear. It was liquor that he had taken from people he had arrested for one reason or another. He looked around among the bottles and chose a bottle of brandy. He glanced around to see if anyone was watching, removed the lid from the bottle and took a long drink. He wiped his mouth on his shirt, placed the bottle back in the trunk and closed the lid. He stood smoking a cigarette and was thinking of the fingers that the young lady at the dry cleaners had thought she had found. He shrugged his shoulders and flipped his cigarette into the weeds. He heard laughter down by the Boo River.

Willie Alexander held the jar containing Clyde Anderson's penis high in the air and laughed as he shook the jar. The two boys who sat on the bank of the river with him seemed fascinated by the contents of the alcohol-filled container. Jimmy Barrett stood and watched the ritual and thought they were admiring a jar of moonshine. He knew the boys often drank beer, but he couldn't figure out where they had gotten moonshine. There had not been any in the locality since Joe Morgan went to prison. Jimmy Barrett walked around behind a line of bushes that filed down the bank toward the river. He crept along silently until he was within a few yards of the trio. Jimmy jumped through the bushes and shouted, "Don't anybody move, you're all under arrest!"

Willie Alexander tossed the jar into the air and threw his hands up as he saw the police chief. The jar landed some four feet out in the water. The other two boys kept their hands down, but they cowered motionless at the edge of the river. Jimmy Barrett blocked their escape route and stood with his hands on his hips. "Now, I want one of you boys to fetch me that jar in the water there. Be careful you don't break it. You!" he pointed at one of the boys nearest the water, "get in there and get me that jar."

The young man looked at Willie Alexander for instructions. Willie said, "We do not have anything to do with that jar. We found it right here on the bank, didn't we fellas?"

Jimmy Barrett took his nightstick from its holster and patted it on his palm. "I told you to get that jar outa there boy. Now get it."

The young man waded out, picked up the jar, and brought it back to shore, meekly handing it to Jimmy Barrett. The police chief held the jar aloft and shook it. He expected to see the bubbling beads form on the top of a jar of moonshine. He held the jar silently aloft for a second or two and then drew it nearer eye level. "Holy shit," he said.

Dr. John Friend sat and looked at his collection of human parts in jars on his desk. First the fingers and now this mysterious penis. Jimmy Barrett had come into his office holding the jar aside as if it contained a black widow spider. He had let Willie Alexander and the boys go home. He didn't fully believe their story of finding the jar, but he could think of no other possible way they could have come by it. He told them he might want to talk to them again. Jimmy Barrett had brought the jar to Dr. Friend, and they had puzzled over the origin of it for an hour. They had called Windfield Waycross to ask if the body they had found had been buried with its penis. Windfield had sputtered and stammered, finally admitting that he wasn't absolutely sure. He was almost sure, but he didn't want to promise them a penis if there was not one on the body if and when it was exhumed. He had declined an offer to look at the penis and had hung up in considerable despair over the whole chain of events.

Dr. John Friend sat, rubbed his pocket watch with his thumb and considered his involvement in all of this. He knew about the fingers. That would involve him with covering up evidence. He had a personal opinion that the body they had found was Friedman. He had no hard medical evidence to back up that assumption, and so he was stuck with the knowledge of the fingers in the coat. If he turned the information over to the state police, he would spend hours in a courtroom listening to the State trying to convict a nutty, middle-aged pharmacy clerk of desecrating the body of an employer now deceased. John Friend picked up the jar containing the penis. "Now, what the hell would Maude want with the body of Friedman? What the hell would she want with his penis if she got rid of the body?" he thought. Even with his knowledge of the mysterious attraction sex held for human beings, he could not reason with Maude Primm's actions.

Maude Primm took her tranquilizers and stayed out of sight more. Gloria Strong took her pep pills and talked incessantly at the Main Street Diner. Mitch the wino rambled on with his monologue. Mrs. John Friend fought against the temptation to take her medicine. Dodd Givens chased his pig. And life in Woodmont Coves yawned into summer.

I loved the summer in Woodmont Coves. There was a noise about summer that I liked. It was a hammering or sawing in the distance. There was also an insectlike hum that couldn't be traced to any exact spot, just a quiet hum that was always present, but one that you never really became accustomed to or oblivious of. The adventures of birds never stopped. They flew, built nests, raised their young and sang the whole summer. The sawing and hammering was always just far enough away to be entertaining. It never occurred to me to go and see what might have been under construction that caused such constant activity. It was a music of the summer, and I was content just to listen.

Mitch and I sat against the dealership wall and ate apples and cheese and small cans of peas. Picnics by the river were never mentioned, as neither of us felt qualified to organize the adventure in the style that Clyde had. The wine Mr. Van Alexander gave us was supposed to be divided equally now. Mitch drank mine, too. He would give me two of the four bottles and then place them all in his shed after we had sat admiring them for a while. I made the trips to the liquor store. I am sure that Mitch made some trips on his own, but I suppose it was when I was away from the dealership. I gave him five dollars a week from the money Clyde had left me, and it seemed an endless supply. I kept it in my salve bag and carried the bag with me at all times. Mitch's depression had lessened with the coming of summer. We were summer people.

I made my customary trips to the bus station for reading material. I watched the newspapers for a notice that The Laughing Man would be performing, but there was never any news.

I occasionally unloaded trucks at Givens' Hardware Store. It was on one such occasion that I saw my mother. She surprised me both in appearance and attitude. She called my name in a bright, crisp voice that I didn't remember hearing before. "James, come here."

I was standing with my back to her. I whirled around to see who had called me and saw my mother standing thirty pounds lighter and wearing high heels. I stood and gaped at her for a few seconds before she called me again. "Come here, James."

I said "Yes, ma'am."

She was standing holding a dark brown suitcase in her hand. It had a pin missing from one of the handle swivels, and she was asking Mr. Givens if he could find a part and fix it. I walked toward her from the rear of the store. She took me to one side and said, "James, how are you? You look healthy enough for a boy who prefers to live out of doors. I am going to be leaving town in a few days, and I hope you'll remember to occasionally check up on your father. He has some nervous habits, and you should get by there once in a while to check up on his welfare."

"Where are you going?" I asked.

"I'll be going to Cincinnati for a while. I know how surprised you are to see me in this frame of mind, but it's something you'll get used to. It will not be necessary to write me any more letters. I will write you occasionally from Cincinnati. I'll send the letters by way of your father. You might want to answer the letters, but you will not have to report to me in writing anymore. You will find that I am quite capable of conversation, and you may communicate with me in that fashion on my return."

I stood motionless, shocked at the clear red color of my mother's hair. The gray was gone. She was smartly dressed in a green tailored suit and a pastel yellow blouse. Her high-heeled shoes were a brown patent leather, and she wore a silver pin in her lapel. She instructed me to go about my work and turned to Dodd Givens. "I'll leave this here for a few days while you fix it." With that she stepped smartly from the store and headed down the sidewalk toward the pharmacy.

I stood staring at the door that my mother had just exited from. I wondered for a moment if it had been my mother. It was definitely not the woman I had known before and had addressed as such. Again I knew fear.

I hurriedly finished my unloading, picked out a roll of masking tape for my reward and left the store. I wanted to go back to my trailer and think about all that I had seen.

I found my trailer hot and stuffy. I opened the trailer door and propped it open with a bottle. I raised the small window and let the breeze flow through. I sat on the small bed and wondered about the change in my mother. She had been plump and melancholy, to the best of my recollection. I realized that that was not a very good description of one's mother. Maybe it had been this perception that had changed her. I was sure that some great thought had taken place in her life, and I knew that it must eventually change my life, too.

I got up and started to walk around the small trailer. Back and forth, from bath to door. I pulled back my foot and started to kick the shower stall door. I stopped myself just in time. I placed my foot on the floor and fell back on the little bed. I sat on the bed and put my hands under my knees and pulled myself into a ball. I was shaking uncontrollably. There was half a bottle of vodka in a drawer under the bed. I managed to get it out and drink several swallows of the hot, burning liquid. The heat from the trailer had almost boiled the vodka. I settled back on the bed and began to calm down. It was several minutes before I was able to sit still. I drank more of the vodka and assessed the situation as being wrong.

The Laughing Man could be seen through the window of the motel. He sat hunched over a table reading a book. It was a book bound in what appeared to be black leather. He would read the book for a minute and then he would jump to his feet and begin walking around the room slapping his hands together and wiping perspiration from his brow. Occasionally he would clasp his hands together and stare at the ceiling in rapture. Then he would quickly return to the book and begin flipping pages as fast as he could read. He was not laughing.

The new Mrs. (Buffet) Friend sat with one sun-tanned knee protruding from under her robe and did her nails. Dr. John Friend sat with his .38 caliber revolver resting against his temple. Buffet Friend suddenly jumped to her feet and yelled, "Boooooo!"

John Friend laid the pistol aside quietly and looked at her in anger. "That's dangerous."

"I've always known it was dangerous. Anytime you try that suicide therapy in my presence, I'm going to startle you with something. Maybe you'll blow your brains out and get your wish."

Buffet Friend sat back in her chair and continued to do her nails. John Friend walked to the small window at the end of the living room and stared out into the leaves of the tree that blocked the view of the street. "I'm happy here, Buffet. These people are strange—I'll grant you that—but this is a good town and these people need a doctor."

He was interrupted by Buffet Friend's slamming down a book. "Sure, you're happy here. You can retire to Switzerland with your money. Me? I'm stuck here doing flower decorations and washing your linen. Well, John, those days are over. I'm only thirty-eight years old. I'm too young to die. I'm too young to sit here in this mad little burg and be murdered or desecrated by some mad mountain woman or man with a rifle."

"There are a few instances of that sort of thing in every community in the world. It is not peculiar to Woodmont Coves."

"I am no longer interested in what's peculiar to Woodmont Coves. I am now interested in what's peculiar. This town is peculiar. You have a man's penis in your office right now. You have no idea whose it is or where it came from. By any standard of sanity that's crazy."

"I know where it came from now. It's a rare case of depravation. It's not part of Woodmont Coves' society."

"Any normal disposition of any kind would be the rare exception in this town, and you know it."

John Friend was tired of defending Woodmont Coves. It was hard to make a point, let alone a case, for it. He closed his office door and sat down on the examining table. He had been watching Buffet Friend for over a month now. It was a crash diet as he had never seen a crash diet. She ate bran and drank water; she took vitamins; she exercised and sunbathed; she shopped and changed her hairstyle once a week. It was the most singular endeavor that he had ever witnessed in a human being. Maybe it was premature menopause. Maybe it was a mental illness of some kind. Perhaps she would suddenly crack. John Friend shrugged his shoulders and picked up his jacket for his evening stroll to the Main Street Diner.

One would think that Dr. Friend would have made some reactionary plans in response to his wife's new disposition and style. He did not. The pistol therapy he had learned from Dan Carter, a close friend in medical school, left him free to pursue his everyday pleasures in life. It was a kind of mad determination to exist and participate in a society he considered out of balance and out of touch with reality. He treasured some moments. He had long ago found the secret—if it was a secret—of letting things regulate themselves. Dr. Friend even practiced his medicine with the theory of self-regulation.

And so it was that Dr. Friend strolled leisurely up Hill Avenue toward the Main Street Diner. He knew Gloria Strong would be there. He knew she was hooked on amphetamines. He also knew that amphetamines were good for colds and hay fever. For a moment Dr. Friend thought he might ask Gloria if she had been having any hay fever or cold symptoms. He dismissed the thought as silly and cynical, even though research and theory were part of every doctor's natural bent.

As he walked, he tried to analyze his wife's actions of late. It was not really all that unusual, he thought. Women had several personalities and could make drastic changes in appearance and disposition if they so desired. He also knew that there was an end to it. His wife would eventually make some declaration of defiance or reach a decision. There was plenty of money. He was not a spending man.

Dr. Friend noticed his shoes as he walked along Hill Avenue. They were soft black shoes often worn by older men with orthopedic problems. He had found them to be comfortable and serviceable. He wondered if people knew how much time a doctor spends on his feet. Pictures of doctors usually showed them sitting behind a desk or on the edge of a bed. He acknowledged that doctors spent much of their lives on their feet. He was pleased with his soft black shoes. He noticed that the birds in Woodmont Coves were seeking sleeping places in the trees that lined the quiet streets.

The Main Street Diner was full. Dr. Friend walked past the window and looked in to see Gloria Strong whisking from table to table carrying dishes of food to the customers. He admired her efficiency for a minute and then decided to walk around the block. He was not sure where he was going, except for a walk. He didn't really want to go back to his home and office. Mrs. Buffet Friend had stopped cooking several weeks ago, and Dr. Friend was in the habit of having dinner at the diner. He was out later than usual this evening, and the diner had filled up.

The doctor walked down Main Street, turned right on Market and right again on First. Reverend Bill Turner stood on the steps of the Woodmont Coves First Methodist Church with his hands grasping the lapels of his suit. "Hello, Dr. Friend. Out for a walk?"

"I was going to have dinner, but the diner's full," the doctor said honestly.

"Well, it's a nice evening for a stroll."

John Friend kept walking toward the reverend. Bill Turner stepped off the porch of the church and extended his hand toward the doctor. They shook hands and Bill Turner said, "I've been meaning to come around and talk to you about my visit of a while back. Do you have a few minutes to talk?"

"Sure. I can't get a seat in the diner for a few minutes anyway."

Bill Turner gestured for Dr. Friend to enter the church. They walked up the steps, down the main aisle of the church, and entered a small office in back of the pulpit.

Reverend Bill Turner took a seat behind a dark wooden desk and offered Dr. Friend a big soft leather chair across the room. Dr. Friend looked around the office and said, "Well, Bill, you've got a nice place here. I didn't know these church offices had such a businesslike look."

"We have to manage like every other organization," the reverend said. "In fact, we have to be a little more organized than most. We don't pay taxes, but there are a lot of folks who like to check the books." Bill Turner laughed as he said that.

John Friend noticed that Bill Turner was fidgety. "Yes sir, this is a nice office," he said.

"It sure is," replied the reverend. "Dr. Friend, would you care for a sip of brandy?"

John Friend looked up, mildly surprised, and said, "Why, yes, I believe I would like a sip of brandy. Seems like just the right thing before dinner."

Bill Turner reached into a small cabinet behind his desk and took out a round, squat bottle of brandy. He removed two glasses from his desk drawer and poured two full glasses. John Friend said, "Whoa, I believe that's about my limit in that one glass, Bill."

"It's dandy brandy, if you'll excuse the rhyme."

John Friend swirled the brandy around in the glass and took a small sip. To his surprise, Bill Turner drank his in one swallow; he licked his lips, wiped his mouth on his sleeve, and produced a small bottle of breath freshener drops with which he wet his tongue. "It doesn't do to have anything except dust on your breath around here," the reverend said.

Bill Turner, feeling that he had full liberty now, poured another glass of the brandy and drank it in the same fashion as he had the first. He looked at Dr. Friend for approval or admonition. John Friend swirled his drink, sipped on it and settled back in his chair.

Bill Turner said, "You know, Dr. Friend, you and I had a discussion a few weeks ago about faith, about having a practical one. I thought about that and, to tell you the truth, I thought you'd be the last person in this country to have any idea how this place works." He gestured around the office. "I read my Bible; it's a good book; it's got the message in it. But it won't work out the way churches are organized these days. Why, I'd have to throw ninety percent of these people right out of here if this were the Lord's church. You know what I mean? These people have no more idea of religion than anything. It's like a social club here." Bill Turner poured another glass of brandy and offered one to John Friend, who declined. Bill Turner went on. "Oh, I might be exaggerating a little. I don't know. Some of these people have the evangelical zeal it takes to make a real church, but they're considered fuddy-duddy, if you know what I mean. You say this office looks like an office? That's exactly what it is. I spend as much time running a business here as I do studying the word of the Lord. I swear I do—on the book, I mean." Reverend Turner sat back in his chair and laughed a loud, honest laugh. "You know what I started to do right before I came to see you?" he asked. "I was going to get up in the pulpit one Sunday morning and tell these people exactly how the Bible stacked up against these softball teams, bingo games, national loyalty committees, and so forth. I shudder to think what would have happened. I would have either been committed or shot." Bill Turner laughed again. "I don't know."

John Friend sensed the frustration that Bill Turner felt. He sipped his brandy and said, "Well Bill, the Church does a lot of good. I mean a *lot* of good. There are people who need the Church a lot more than they need my medicine. If we didn't have churches, we'd need a lot more mental health clinics in this country. You do more good than you realize. The Church is an important part of this society, and I'd be the last person to scorn it."

"Oh, I know that," Bill Turner said. "I'm a pro. I know what I'm doing. It's just that a man must have a purpose in life. I'll tell you the truth. I didn't know it was going to be like this when I was in the seminary. They hinted at it a lot. They made jokes about it. We were told how to raise money. They told us how to promote. And yet, under all that surface, whiz-bang business line, there was still the dedication to the Almighty that got me through it." Bill Turner took another drink of the brandy and laughed again. "You know something, Doc, there are a lot of pretty women who come to churches. There's something about a God-fearing woman that makes them even more attractive. Did you know that?" Bill Turner was talking to himself by now. He slapped his hand across his leg and said, "I'll tell you, my wife thinks she's got more of the Lord in her than the Pope. She wraps herself up in these committees and things and just disappears from the face of the earth. She thinks I'm Billy Graham or somebody. I know my way around the church business. I'll tell you that."

Bill Turner got up from his desk and came over to sit on the edge of the desk in front of Dr. Friend. He said, "I'm gonna tell you something. I had this girl, Gloria Strong, at the Main Street Diner come down here the other night. She said she had had a vision of some sort and was counting on me to interpret it for her. Said she had seen a day—now I can tell you this, Doc—when men of the cloth would be freed from their sexual hang-ups—yes, that was it—and would be able to take from life what they wanted and needed. I can't tell you how wrought up she was. I tell you it's happened to me before. I mean, women get their preacher and their lovers all mixed up sometimes. You know what I mean? I can't turn anybody away from this church. That's one thing even the elders agree with. We don't encourage these excited people to upset the church any, but we don't turn 'em away." Bill Turner looked at John Friend for some sort of reaction.

John Friend finished his brandy and stood. He put his hand on Bill Turner's shoulder and said, "I'm sure the problems of the church are many. I admire the work you do. I've got to have some dinner now."

Bill Turner followed John Friend up the aisle of the church and out onto the steps while explaining his problems. "I'm just gonna handle these things one day at a time, Doc. I see no reason to turn people away from here because I don't agree with the way they see things. Take care of yourself, and let me know if any of your patients ever need me for anything. Just call me, hear?"

John Friend walked back up to the Main Street Diner and ordered a salad and a small piece of beef.

John Friend ate the salad, some of the potatoes that came with the meal, and absentmindedly pushed the beef aside and sipped his coffee. He assumed that the brandy had dulled his appetite and did not consider the rejection of the beef to be a part of a doctor's subconscious distaste for meat.

Gloria Strong was clearing the tables now. The dinner rush was over, and there were only two or three people in the diner. Gloria had largely ignored John Friend since he had cut off her supply of pills. She put a stack of dishes on the service window counter and sat down to read the Bible. She was sitting on a stool by the cash register, pausing to reflect on what she had just read, as if she were preparing for an exam. Dr. John Friend was sitting within speaking range, so he said, "Are you teaching Sunday school, Gloria?"

Gloria looked at the doctor with a beatific smile. "I've found Go-ahd," she said quietly. "I've found what I have been searching for. I have found the answer to it all."

John Friend was startled to hear her say the word God. She had somehow put an *a* in it, and it sounded as if she were saying Go-ahd. He had heard other preachers and clergymen use pronunciation like that, but it sounded strange coming from Gloria Strong. The way the word was pronounced signaled something to him that he couldn't quite analyze.

Gloria Strong was not wearing makeup. Her pretty

red hair was tied behind her neck, and she was wearing flat shoes and rather dark hose. She went back to reading her Bible and was interrupted by one of the customers calling for more coffee. John Friend could hear her talking in a sweet evangelical voice to the people at the table down the aisle. He left his money on the table with his food ticket and walked to the door. As he closed the door to the diner behind him he heard Gloria Strong say in her new, quiet voice, "Go-ahd bless you, Doctor."

John Friend walked down to the light that shone from the corridor of the River City Bank. He stood there in the light and admired his shoes again. He looked skyward and wondered if there were some astrological reasoning for the change in the women in his life. John Friend believed in cycles. He wondered again about Reverend Turner's religion.

Back in his small office, John Friend took the two jars containing the penis and the fingers from the shelf and sat staring at them. He put a tape on his playback machine and adjusted his earphones to listen to a recorded lecture on women and menopause.

I don't know how many days I was in my trailer. I was taking the pills that my father had given me, and I slept a lot. I do remember that one afternoon I was half asleep and half awake. I met The Singing Girl. There was a swing set in the trailer park. Some of the people who lived in the park let their children play there. There were two swings side by side on the iron bar, which was supported by strong metal posts set in concrete. The grass under the swings was worn down, and the dust would fly in the afternoon sun as the feet of the children touched the ground while swinging. I was sitting under one of the trees in the trailer park. I didn't see The Singing Girl arrive; she was suddenly there, swinging in one of the swings and singing in a low, sweet voice. Her hair was a long, black, fluffy mass of silk. Her skin was an even, deep-textured golden brown. She wore a white airy dress with a floral pattern. Her face was expressionless. Her mouth was wide, and her lips were full. Her nose seemed to be sculpted by some ancient master. There was no dust under the swing. She appeared to be moved by some outside force. Back and forth, back and forth, with a rhythm that complemented her song. She sang:

> "Words, words, words, words, words, words
> Words, words, words, words, words, words
> Words, words, words, words, words, words
> Words, words, words, words, words, words"

It was so beautiful, so perfect, so melodic. I sat for over an hour and listened as she sang. I tried to arouse myself and speak to her. I tried to applaud this beautiful girl and her beautiful song. I could not move. It was as if I had been frozen for the performance. I expected the swing to slow down and stop for lack of some propelling force. It did not. The song grew more meaningful and more beautiful.

> "Words, words, words, words, words, words
> Words, words, words, words, words, words"

I began to hum along with the song, "HUM hum HUM hum HUM hum HUM hum." The Singing

Girl heard my humming and turned to smile at me. Her teeth were black and yellow and rotten. I felt the jar to my system. My whole body and mind felt as if I had been electrocuted. I managed to get to my feet and started to run toward the dealership. I was almost at the laundromat before the singing ceased in my ears:

"Words, words, words, words . . ."

Mitch was sitting on his Indian blanket when I turned into the dealership. I stood and looked at him for a minute before walking over and taking a seat beside him. I gathered my knees in my arms and breathed heavily in the warm sun. Mitch started moving his feet in rhythm. He started it:

"HUM hum HUM hum HUM . . ."

I put my hand, palm out, toward Mitch and he stopped. I got to my feet, went to the edge of the street and looked up and down Hill Avenue, I turned to Mitch and motioned to him. Mitch rolled over on his stomach, got to his feet by way of his hands and knees, and ambled toward me.

As we walked down Hill Avenue to Second Street and the liquor store, Mitch mumbled one of his monologues:

"Dey's some dat make da day aw rite and some don't
Make da day as best you can and be cool
Da sun ain't be waitin' fo you to move
Jus say 'Moooooorninn Man'"

I said, "Mooooorninn Man." Mitch bounced up and down in agreement.

I bought two good-sized bottles of sloe gin at the liquor store. Mitch stood behind me and bounced around. I had no idea where he had acquired this new movement. It was a happy kind of bounce which was generated from the waist up. His head would bounce up and down as if he were listening to some music in his head.

We went back up Hill Avenue carrying our two bottles of sloe gin wrapped in brown paper bags. When we got to the dealership Mitch wanted to stop, but I got on his left side and sort of nudged him past, gesturing toward the park. We arrived at the trailer park and stood at the edge of the parking area where we could see the swing set. There was a small boy kicking up dust at the swing. The boy would yell out in excited pleasure as he reached the apogee of the arc. Mitch stood silent and restless beside me for a minute and then turned and started back down Hill Avenue. I followed him, removing the lid from the bottle of sloe gin and taking a long, sweet drink.

Mitch and I were nearly finished with our bottles when we saw the woman coming across the gravel parking area of the dealership. Mitch noticed the swift, determined walk of the woman and started half-crawling, half-walking toward his shed. There was an air of immediacy in the stride of the woman. She was slender and of average height. She wore sneakers and jeans topped off with a bright blue blouse. Her hair was tied back in a ponytail effect, and she wore matching blue jewelry and carried a brown leather fringed bag across her shoulder. It was my mother.

Dear Mother,
   I have heard that you have . . .

The letter was interrupted by the bright voice of my mother. "James, James, James . . . look at you. What on earth will you come to? And drinking!"

I stood and looked at my mother and stared at her costume and her stance. She had her hands on her hips. She talked for several minutes in a bright, clear, admonishing tone. I heard her say she had gotten a job in Middletown. I heard her say she would be working in public relations for a very worthy cause. She would not be going to Cincinnati—there were memories. She stumbled only when she mentioned she would not be living with my father anymore. I sat speechless as she whirled and marched around the corner. I knew it to be the work of The Doctor Who Hated Fear. He had done things like this before. He had made my mother fifteen years younger and had given her a job in Middletown for some worthy cause. He had dressed her in modern clothes and had taken the gray from her hair. He had brightened her step and cleared her voice. He had given her the gift of youth and had told her to leave my father. I took another drink from the bottle of sloe gin and saw The Doctor Who Hated Fear's huge truck pull up to the edge of the curb near the dealership. He jumped from the truck and said, "James, my boy, you are next. We are going to explain something to you once and for all." The Doctor Who Hated Fear waved his hand and a large stage appeared in front of me. He waved his hand again and a choir stood on the stage. The choir was singing:

"Words, words, words, words, words, words"

He waved his hand again and a long black limousine pulled alongside the edge of the stage. Jesus stepped from the limousine dressed in a dark three-piece suit. He wore a red and white striped tie, a pale blue shirt, and a lot of diamond-studded rings. Jesus was clean-shaven and his hair had been trimmed like a movie star's. Jesus stepped up to the stage and began to wave the Bible in the air as he preached. Jesus preached things that I had heard from the Bible. The choir chanted:

"Words, words, words, words, words, words"

The Doctor Who Hated Fear came to me and whispered even as Jesus preached, "Now, you see, Jesus is just like us. He was once an ordinary man. Are you afraid of him now?"

I looked at all I saw before me and said calmly, "More so now than ever."

The Doctor Who Hated Fear stomped his foot and the earth shook as the scene vanished from the gravel lot. "You have no sense of what we are all about, James. You are ignorant beyond words." The Doctor Who Hated Fear jumped back into his huge truck and disappeared in a cloud of dust.

Mitch and I finished our bottles of sloe gin and made another trip to the liquor store. On the way back we stopped at Strong's Supermarket and bought a large can of chicken and dumplings. It was late afternoon when we sat and heated the can of food over the hubcap we kept for that purpose. As the Sterno burned down to a flicker, Mitch produced two forks from the shed and we sat and ate in silence and contentment.

I spent the night on Clyde's side of the shed. I was somehow afraid to go back to the trailer, and there was no good reason to go anyway.

Next morning I awoke and found dew on my feet where I had wrestled with the thin bedding and wound up with my feet protruding from under the shed. The morning was bright and clear, and the sounds of summer were all around. I sat holding my head for a few minutes, trying to plan my day. Mitch was sitting outside against the side of the building, hammering on his shoe with a piece of wood. There must have been a nail out of place because he would occasionally raise the shoe and look inside to find the offensive sharp edge. He seemed content to have a project for the morning, so I took my salve bag and went back to the trailer for some clean clothes and took a trip to the paint factory showers.

I found the trailer park silent and empty. I thought back to the previous day and The Singing Girl's song. I shook the memory from my head and gathered clean clothes and stuffed them into my salve bag.

I went to the paint factory, walking down Main Street and turning left on Market Street to avoid seeing my mother or father. I realized it was Saturday when I saw that the guard was not at the gate and the gate was locked. It never mattered that the gates to the paint factory showers were locked on Saturdays. All one had to do to get in was move a section of the fence, insert a stick or a nail into the side door latch and walk in. I assumed the place was left available under this pretense of security for insurance reasons.

I switched on the bright fluorescent lights overhead and placed my salve bag on one of the redwood benches that lined the walls. I undressed and reached into the shower stall, turned on the water, and adjusted it to a comfortable temperature. I stepped inside the shower stall, closed the white curtain, and stood luxuriating in the caressing water. I was humming The Singing Girl's song when a hand reached into the shower and grabbed one of the fixtures. HUM hum HUM hum . . . I suddenly let out a scream as scalding hot water splashed against my chest and down my body. If I remember well, I jumped from the shower and banged my head on the side of the door while getting out. I fell against the far wall of the room and onto my salve bag and my clothes, which were piled up on a bench. Willie Alexander stood snapping a wet towel at my already burning feet and legs. He was chanting some sort of childish taunt. I got up off the bench with my knife in hand. I had opened the blade and was waving it toward him. As I neared him, he lashed out at me with the wet towel. The knife blade caught his hand as he swung the towel, and the white, fluffy cotton was suddenly colored a lurid, bright red. Willie Alexander screamed as he dropped the towel and grabbed one hand in the other. The room rang with his voice as he yelled, "He's got a knife . . . run!"

The two young boys who were with him stood in a state of panic by the wall near the side door. They grabbed their clothes, piled on one of the benches, and ran into one another as the trio, all naked, made it through the door and onto the gravel pathway outside the building. They hobbled and groaned over the rough gravel, clinging to their clothes, and looking back to see if I was in pursuit with the knife.

I stood in the middle of the floor and started an oriental war-type dance with the knife. I shouted loudly, "HE-YAHH, HE-YAHH, HE-YAHH!" I danced from one foot to the other and swung the knife through the moist air in the shower room. It was instantly silent. I stood still and attentive for any sound indicating that the three might return. All I could hear were the nice sounds of summer. Birds sang their little songs; insects murmured at their work, and somewhere in the distance someone hammered and sawed.

I found that most of the burning sensation had been centered on my knees and feet. I had reacted to the scalding water quickly enough to protect my shoulders and my middle. I dabbed the soft towels on the stinging red skin of my knees and feet. I got a fresh towel from the rack and used my feet to shuffle along on the towel and mop up the little trail of blood that led to the side door. I threw all of the bloody, wet towels in the large stainless steel bin, got dressed and made my way back to the hole in the fence. I was well on my way back to the trailer when Jimmy Barrett came down Market Street with sirens going and lights flashing. I stood with my hands over my ears as he slammed on the brakes and jumped from the car. He spoke several words to me before he realized that I could not hear him. He reached up and jerked my hands away from my ears and said, "James you're under arrest for . . . er . . . uh . . . well . . . you're under arrest. You can make a phone call to your father, but you won't need to do that because he already knows. So get in the car."

I started to get into the front seat. Jimmy Barrett grabbed me and pushed me into the back. I sat there as he readjusted his police gear and got into the driver's seat. I noticed there were no window or door handles in the back of the car. Jimmy Barrett and I were separated by a metal-mesh window. With an instinct that I wondered about later, I reached into the salve bag, took out the knife and hid it under the seat.

My father was sitting in the police station reading a small book. He stood and stretched and frowned when we entered the room. Willie Alexander and the two boys who had been with him sat frightened in the brightly lit, cluttered room. Jimmy Barrett motioned for me to sit in a seat beside my father. He had a legal pad in his hand and was making notes of some kind. He looked up from his pad and said, "Now, let's get this story straight. Willie, you say James attacked you with a knife, is that right?"

I quickly and innocently replied, "I don't have a knife."

Willie Alexander said, "Yeah, he attacked us with a knife."

"He made me take off my clothes while he held a shotgun on me!" I shouted.

Jimmy Barrett said, "A shotgun?"

Willie said, "That ain't got nothing to do with this. It was a long time ago." My father's eyes brightened.

"He held a shotgun on me," I said.

"I didn't do that today," Willie said.

"Look here now, let me ask the questions around here," said Jimmy Barrett. "What I want to know is if you all want to press charges against each other. Willie, you say you was cut on the hand. James, you say he had a shotgun. What do you think, Doctor?" Jimmy Barrett looked at my father.

"Well, Willie's hand is not cut bad; it's just a flesh wound. I would recommend that we all forget this matter entirely." My father sighed when he said the words.

Willie Alexander said, "I ain't pressin' no charges."

I said, "I didn't want to come here in the first place."

Jimmy Barrett stood up and folded his note pad. "James, you better give me that knife to keep for a few days." He looked at Willie and said, "What in hell was you doing with a shotgun?"

I told Jimmy Barrett I didn't have a knife, and Willie said that he didn't have a shotgun. The police chief looked at us quizzically and rubbed the back of his neck. He waved his hand at Willie and his friends and said, "You boys get out of here and stay out of trouble. There are laws against certain things, you know." Willie Alexander waved his bandaged hand at us as he left the room.

My father waved a hand at Jimmy Barrett and left the room after the three boys. "Do you have a knife?" he asked.

"No."

"Well, you had one. You'd better be careful with it. The blade is very sharp."

"Where did you get the book you are reading? I've seen it."

He held out a thin volume of *Take the Fear from Your Life*. "Your mother has been reading this book for some time now. I thought I'd skim through it. It's mostly B.S."

I sat and wondered about The Doctor Who Hated Fear. It was his book, and my mother had been reading it. I tried to remember if I had been dreaming or if I had met some of the people I contended with in my life. I stood and said to someone I was sure was my father, "Mother told me everything." I left the room quietly. My father turned his attention to the small book.

I went back to my trailer and sat on my bed while drinking from a bottle of vodka. I looked outside toward the swings in the little playground and saw a man sitting motionless in the seat of one swing. He was dressed all in white. His hair, his shirt, his tie, his suit, his shoes—everything about him was white. I stepped down from the trailer door and approached him from one side. He turned and smiled at me with nice white teeth. "Ho, James. How are you today? The Thinking Man here. What can I do for you?"

"Why are you dressed in white?"

"I am dressed in white so you will talk to me. Do you realize that if I were to dress in black, people would be afraid of me? I dress in white because I do a lot of high thinking, and high thinking takes one into blackness, of course."

"What is the answer to the big question and what is the big question?"

"Ah, you are clever, James. The answer to the big question is made simple by having a small answer. The answer to the big question will be a revelation that will be available at the end. You will snap your fingers and say 'Why didn't I think of that?' when you hear the big question answered." He flipped through the pages of a small white book and said, "Of course you will have to devise the big question, because that is your right. If you do not come up with a genuinely good big question, there will, of course, be no small answer. I don't really expect big questions from people of your sort. Your physical industry is not compatible with high thinking."

"I want to know why I was put here."

"Ho, ho, and ha, ha. What makes you think you were *put* here? I'm afraid that is not high thinking at all. Your small thinking gets you nearer high thinking than high thinking itself. If I were you, I would try to further simplify my small thinking and pick up the curve to high thinking."

"This is a game, isn't it?"

"Oh, goodness yes. You see how well your small thinking brings you near the truth. I must congratulate you. Farewell!" And with that The Thinking Man was gone.

I sat on the steps of my trailer and took off my shoes. I rolled my pants legs up and inspected the pink, tender skin. The burning sensation was gone. The skin was tender to the touch, but I let the cool evening breeze blow across my skin and sipped the vodka. I walked barefoot across the grass to the tree behind the swings. I sat down and clapped my hands together in a loud and stinging way. The Thinking Man appeared in one swing. He turned and glared at me angrily. "What now, James? What now?"

". . . the valley of the shadow of death. Explain that? Is death a shadow, and does it reside in a valley?"

The Thinking Man glared at me again. "Bullshit," he said, and was gone. I looked around to see if anyone else had witnessed this exchange. There was no one around. I slapped my leg and laughed a good, loud, strong, happy laugh.

Words, words, words, words, words, words
Words, words, words, words, words, words

Jimmy Barrett had no way of knowing that there was a knife in the backseat of his police cruiser. He drove sleepily down the streets of Woodmont Coves. He circled the paint factory. He turned right and drove slowly into Hill Avenue. He brightened his lights when he saw a figure move in the darkness. He slowed down and caught sight of someone running from Dr. John Friend's back door. He watched the person carefully. The figure darted from the side of the house and into the bushes. Jimmy Barrett pulled the car to a lurching halt and jumped from the vehicle while drawing his gun from its holster. "Stop or I'll shoot," he shouted. The figure in the bushes stopped, throwing arms and hands into the air. "Come back here. That's a police order!"

The figure walked slowly, arms raised, back toward the car.

As the person neared the car, Jimmy Barrett reached out, grabbing hold of an arm. In the darkness he could not make out any features. He shoved the person into the backseat of the police cruiser and said, "You are under arrest for suspicion of . . . for acting suspicious."

It was quiet on the street when Jimmy Barrett pulled his police car up to the Woodmont Coves Courthouse. He stepped from the front seat of the car and opened the back door. He saw the glint of the knife in the soft glow of the streetlight. There was a rapid, constant swinging of the arm holding the knife. There were flat, ugly, slapping sounds against the chest of Jimmy Barrett, and he felt violated, hurt and angered by what this person was doing to him. Jimmy Barrett spit blood and started to fight back an instant before he fell to the sidewalk—dead.

There were several determined-looking men in gray and black suits in Woodmont Coves the next day. Everyone was questioned about Jimmy Barrett. I was called in to answer questions about the fight I had had with Willie Alexander. I explained that I had not had a knife and that Willie must have cut his hand on something else during the scuffle. There were finger prints taken of every article in the car. Mine were explained by the fact that I had been in the car the day before the slaying. My father looked grim and saddened. He murmured to me that this would not be taken lightly and that we could expect to hear from the investigators again.

At the bus station I picked up a newspaper containing an article which said that Jimmy Barrett was a perfect gentleman in every way:

POLICE CHIEF WAS GOOD MAN
WOODMONT COVES—Friends say Jimmy Barrett, senselessly slain in front of the Woodmont Coves Courthouse last night, was a perfect gentleman in every way. Police and state troopers are searching for the slayer, or slayers, in an intensive investigation. No weapon has been found, however . . .

I spent the weeks during the investigation sitting with Mitch and watching grasshoppers play across the hot, dusty grass that bordered the sides of the dealership buildings. I would often have to go down to the police station to answer questions the severe men in their suits and ties asked. I answered the questions over and over. At one point I said that I had been at my trailer that evening talking to The Thinking Man. There was much talk of the strange man until my father took some of the severe men aside and explained me to them in a fashion that seemed to pacify them. There were reports that a man had been arrested in an adjoining county who carried several knives and had a criminal record. The investigation shifted to that concern for a while. It was two weeks before the severe men packed up piles of papers, reels of tapes, and boxes of photos to return to the state capital.

Life in Woodmont Coves was warm and green and pleasant now. Mitch and I continued to spend the money Clyde had left me. I would go to the Main Street Diner and get quart jars of chili and cups of coleslaw. The chili was spicy and hot, and once I cajoled Mitch to taste it, he loved it. I bought crackers and shared the chili from plastic cups Gloria Strong would give me. I could almost believe that Mitch was gaining weight on chili and coleslaw.

Gloria Strong had taken to wearing an ill-fitting long, thin, black dress. She did not wear makeup, and she did not take her hair from a bun at the nape of her neck. She moved swiftly and assuredly about the diner and spoke in a soft, angelic voice. It all attracted me to her. She lost weight, and her eyes were wide and distant at times.

One evening, after I had returned the quart jar in which she had put chili, I sat staring at her as she worked. She moved around the diner and did all the things required to close an eating establishment. She put the chairs on the tables, emptied the ashtrays, swept and mopped the floors, and turned the card in the doorway so that it read "CLOSED." I sat on one of the stools and watched her move happily and distractedly around the room. She turned to me and said in her new angelic voice, "I'm sorry, James, we're closing now." Her voice was soft, considerate and musical.

I asked, "Where do you go now?"

She turned to me quickly. I thought I could see her breasts bounce and swing as she moved. She paused for a breathless moment and said, "From here I go to pray."

I stood speechless for a moment and then I said, "Can I go with you?"

Gloria looked at me in a puzzled way. "Do you know Jesus?"

"Sure," I said.

She smiled her angelic smile. I thought her breasts moved inside the thin black dress again. "We'll talk to Him together," she said.

Gloria locked the door to the diner and took my hand. "Go-ahd understands," she said.

I suddenly let go of Gloria's hand and asked her to excuse me. I rushed back to the diner and went around the side of the building to where the garbage cans were standing. I reached behind one of the cans for a bottle of vodka. I took a long, slow drink and then another. I put the bottle back behind the cans and rejoined Gloria, who was waiting and staring at stars. Her eyes were wide and pleasant. We started walking, and I thought her breasts moved again.

As we walked up the steps of the Woodmont Coves First Methodist Church I said, "I don't think we're allowed in here at night." (I had been told not to go into the church at night.)

Gloria Strong turned and pressed my hands in hers. "This is the house of the Lord," she said.

We walked slowly and steadily down the main aisle of the church and sat down directly in front of the pulpit. A large statue of Christ high above us was bathed in muted light. I looked at the figure for a minute and realized that it was one of those things that never looked at you—no matter where you are in the room. It made me feel better.

Gloria Strong sat and held my hand and stared straight ahead. She turned and looked at me with her huge, bright eyes. "James, do you know that Maude Primm prayed through Wednesday night?"

"Maude Primm?"

"Yes, it was so beautiful. So beautiful. Reverend Turner says he wants me to pray through. He says I'm not ready just yet. He counsels me privately. He's out of town tonight attending a church business meeting. He's such a great man of the Lord. He says I've helped him understand a lot, too."

"Maude Primm has joined the church and got saved?"

"Yes, and she prayed through Wednesday night. I didn't help because I've not prayed through myself, and so Reverend Turner asked me to stay in the back, where I usually sit, and help her with my private prayers. I guess they do help, though. She prayed through Wednesday night right here in this church. I want to pray through, but Reverend Turner says the Lord works in mysterious ways, and he'll let me know when I'm ready."

Gloria Strong held my hand so tightly it started to perspire. I removed my hand from hers and placed it on her leg. She sighed and patted my hand. I put my hand down under the long, thin dress and moved it up to her knee. She patted my hand. She wasn't wearing anything under the dress, so I moved my hand up between her legs until I felt pubic hair. I sat there silently for a moment. Gloria turned and kissed me on the mouth. I put my right arm around her waist and lowered her to the dark blue carpet. I made love to her as she whispered small prayers and sang small songs. We sat upright in the pew again, and she smoothed her dress and patted my hand. I sat looking at the floor for a long while and then realized that I had to cough. I stifled the cough as long as I could and then got up and walked swiftly to the front of the church and out the door. I coughed and slapped my cheeks with my hand. I took a deep breath of the evening air and walked back to the door of the church. My voice sounded loud and vulgar as I said, "Good-night, Gloria. Thank you."

Van Alexander, the tall, silver-haired, suntanned owner of the Cadillac dealership, sat behind his desk filing his nails. He was a neat, if not meticulous, man in his early fifties. The wide, highly polished cherry wood desk was clear of paperwork. A gold letter opener and a leather-trimmed desk set were all in place as this tall, thin-featured, green-eyed man sat and studied his fingernails. He placed the gold fingernail file he had been using in a small, black leather holder and put it neatly into his top desk drawer.

White, ceiling-to-floor drapes graced the two windows at the rear of the desk. A gold wall-to-wall carpet adorned the floor of the rectangular office. Antiquated color prints depicting scenes of English boar hunting were grouped on the wall to the left of the occupant. Van Alexander had secured an interior decorator from Middletown to make sure his office would be in good taste. He had neither added nor taken away from the decorator's original ideas.

It was said in Woodmont Coves that one could set a clock by the legendary walk that Van Alexander made from his home on Second Street to the dealership each day. The tall, athletic figure would exit from his house and walk briskly, almost militarily, to the rear of the dealership, enter through the side door, and open his office.

When Van Alexander thought that his presence was required at social occasions, he would make his entrance several minutes after the evening had begun, make the rounds, shake the hands of notable guests and then disappear. He was always visible at any important gathering, and yet he was the least controversial man in Woodmont Coves. He donated generously to each political party and gave money to all the noteworthy charities. If it troubled Van Alexander that his son, Willie, was a homosexual, he never voiced it in public. They lived together in the big house on Second Street. Mrs. Alexander had died some ten years earlier, and he and his son had divided the house and lived separate lives. Van Alexander used the front of the house, containing the small living room, first bedroom and the kitchen. A huge den door separated the oversized den and small kitchenette where his son lived. It was a convenient arrangement. Van Alexander never entered his son's part of the house, and Willie never entered the front part. The furniture in the large upstairs area and the spacious back rooms was covered with sheets, and the doors stayed closed.

On the one occasion that Van Alexander had peeked into his son's quarters, he had seen a wide mattress on the floor, pictures of male movie stars and singers on the wall, and a collection of rocks and wood pieces stacked along the bookshelves by the fireplace.

Van Alexander picked up the phone and dialed the number of Dr. John Friend. He let the phone ring six times and hung up. He dialed again, and this time Gloria Strong answered the phone at the Main Street Diner. "Diner."

"Is Dr. Friend there, please?"

"Yes, one minute."

Van Alexander could hear the handpiece of the phone tapping against the wall of the diner where Gloria Strong had left it hanging while she told Dr. Friend of the call. John Friend answered the phone in a grumbling way. "Dr. Friend here. What is it?"

"This is Van, John. Need to talk to you a few minutes."

"Oh, sure, Van." John Friend's voice brightened. "Want to come by my office?"

"Well, I thought you might drop by here a minute. How's your book today?"

"Oh, it's full, as usual, but I'll stop in. Say ten minutes?"

"Good. I'll see you here."

John Friend walked quickly up Hill Avenue. He didn't know why he hurried. It seemed there was a hint of urgency in Van Alexander's voice. And after he thought about it, he decided it was a little unusual for Alexander to request anyone to come to his office. He mused over the call as he paced down the short block to the dealership.

Van Alexander reached into his top desk drawer and retrieved the pretty four-bladed knife with a gold star embedded in the dark-brown wooden handle. He heard a knock at his office door and assumed it to be John Friend. "Come in, come in," he called in a loud voice. John Friend entered the room and closed the door behind him. He shook hands with Van Alexander and was motioned over to a soft leather chair.

Van Alexander turned his back to John Friend and stared out the window behind his desk. "John, I'll get right to the point."

He reached down and turned back the corners of the handkerchief that covered the murder weapon on his desk. "My son, Willie, killed Jimmy Barrett with this."

John Friend sat motionless for a minute and then slowly raised himself to his feet. He stared at the knife on the desk. "Are you sure?" he asked. "Are you absolutely, positively, beyond a doubt *sure*?"

Van Alexander nodded his head. John Friend moved closer to look at the knife. "Fingerprints?" he asked.

Van Alexander said, "I'm sure there will be. I picked up the knife in that handkerchief."

John Friend returned to his seat. Van Alexander sat down at his desk and put his head in his hands. He sighed a deep sigh.

John Friend said, "Tell me how it happened."

Van Alexander explained:

"Willie called me the night of the murder. It must have been after midnight. I was asleep. He said he was at a friend's house and had a flat tire. He wanted me to come and get him. He sounded drunk. I told him it was the middle of the night and that if he'd spend the night there I'd send somebody out to get him. He sounded very drunk or on drugs. He called me a dirty name and said he would walk. He hung up on me, and I kinda woke up and figured I'd go get him. Jimmy Barrett beat me to him. I pulled over to the side of the road and watched him get Willie. I thought he'd probably take him to the house, so I turned around and went back home. I was in the driveway and saw them pass me and go on toward the police station. I thought I'd better get him out, so I drove by there and saw them fighting on the street. I pulled over and parked there by the railroad and started to get out and go over there and stop them. Jimmy Barrett fell to the sidewalk, and Willie came running across the street toward Market Street. I was sitting there with my lights out; I don't think he even saw me. He almost threw the knife at my car. I guess he just wanted to get rid of it. I got out and got the knife and went on home. People started to gather up at the Woodmont Coves Courthouse. Willie was dressed in women's clothes, and he was swinging the black wig he had while he was running. It was the craziest scene I've ever seen. I guess I'll remember it as long as I live. I just . . ."

John Friend pursed his lips and stared at the floor. He said, "They'll want to know why you lied about it before. They'll want to know why you didn't come forward with the story and the knife."

"I'll tell them the truth. He's my son, you know. Can a father testify against his son?"

"Yes."

Van Alexander turned and stared out the window again. "You know, John, I am afraid of Willie. I always have been. Since his mother's death we've been in two different worlds. He's mean and vicious. He has called me names on the various occasions I've tried to talk to him. He's almost thirty. He gets a paycheck here at the dealership. I'm afraid of him."

I was at the bus station looking for something to read when I saw the newspaper headline:

ALEXANDER GETS LIFE FOR SLAYING POLICE CHIEF

There was a picture of a wild Willie Alexander being led from the Woodmont Coves Courthouse by police. Jimmy Barrett stared out from the front page with a boyish grin. His picture was framed in black. I studied the photos a minute and decided each of them should be framed in black.

Willie had screamed his innocence when confronted with the evidence. He was defiant to the end of the short trial and sentencing. There was a picture of the murder weapon on the inside of the newspaper. I sat in the bus station staring at the photo of the pretty knife with a star embedded in the dark-brown wooden handle.

As I was walking up Market Street later that afternoon I noticed that there were carpenters and painters remodeling the den of the Alexander place. It seemed the right thing for a neat and orderly person like Van Alexander to be doing.

I walked back toward the dealership and saw a skeeterbug used for hauling pulpwood screech to a halt as it passed me on the street. The driver backed the vehicle up to where I was standing, and Mose Random said, "Hello there, James. I didn't say Jim but James." He laughed a loud laugh that made me glad to see him. I walked over and shook his hand. He said, "What happened to you that night in Middletown? Boy, you flipped out there for a minute."

"I think I just had too much to drink. It was an adventure, though."

Mose Random ran his fingers through his black curly beard. "I'm kinda looking for a partner in some crime."

"How's that?"

"Well, I've got a couple of girls lined up for tomorrow night. I'm gonna take 'em to see Mo Jumpsum at The Starlite Club in Middletown. You wanna go?"

"What's Mo Jumpsum do?"

"Hey, you don't know Mo Jumpsum? Where you been? On the moon?"

"I don't know him."

"He's got the best band you ever heard. If you want to go I can get you a date with Blondie's friend. You 'member Blondie?"

"I remember her, yes."

"Well, you gotta have a tie to get in the place. But if you wanna go I'll pick you up—right here's as good a place as any—tomorrow about two o'clock in the after-noon."

"You have to wear a tie?"

"Well, it's a pretty nice place. They try to keep the riffraff out."

"Okay, I'll see you here tomorrow at two."

Mose Random shook my hand with both of his hands and jerked his head in agreement with our plans. "Be here at two sharp."

With that he threw the old skeeterbug into gear and rattled off down the street.

On my way back to my trailer I saw Maude Primm and Gloria Strong walking toward the door of the Woodmont Coves First Methodist Church.

I sat up far into the evening eating chili and coleslaw and reading a Western. I slept late the next morning and awoke to realize that it was a Saturday. I could tell Saturdays because there weren't the morning noises of people going to work and to school. I could hear the children playing on the swing set in the trailer park. I felt as good as I had felt in years. It was unusually warm in the trailer, so I opened the small window and the door to create a breeze. The old lady who ran the trailer park waved at me when she passed. I sang out, "Goooooood morning."

I remembered that Mose Random and I had plans for the day, and it made me feel good to know that there was an adventure in the works. It was a pretty sunlit morning in Woodmont Coves. I treasured the quiet moment. The fat man who worked at the carnival during the Strawberry Festival had left half a pack of cigarettes in one of the small drawers in the trailer. I took the pack from the drawer and lit one of the cigarettes and puffed on it and watched the smoke curl out into the fresh summer air. I had not smoked before, but it seemed the sane and sensible thing to do. I felt cultured and relaxed. I felt completely normal, and there was a kind of joy in the experience.

The cigarette began to irritate my mouth, so I dipped the end of it in a half-filled glass of water and threw it out the door. I gathered my salve bag and my clean clothes and headed downtown. Mose Random had said I would need a tie for the evening.

There was a huge, gruff, dark man in the Son 'n' Dad Clothing Store. I bought a light blue shirt, a dark blue sportcoat with gold buttons, and asked for a maroon tie. I explained to him that I could not make a knot. He marched off into the back of the store and came back with a shorter, lighter tie with a clip at the top. He removed the cellophane from the shirt and showed me how the clip went in front of the neck and the corners of the tie fit under the collar. After paying for the things I had bought, I noticed that the money Clyde had left me was getting low. I had not thought I would ever spend so much money so soon. The layer of bills in the little bag was thin now. I thanked the grumpy, dark man and left the store. As I walked from the store, the man leaned one elbow on the counter, put his chin in his hand and stared off into the distance. He seemed like an awfully big man to be selling clothes.

I showered quickly at the paint factory. I was excited about how I would look in the new clothes, especially a tie. I used one end of a towel to clean my shoes. There were no full-length mirrors in the shower room, but I was pleased with myself when I could see the shirt, tie and part of the coat. I put my things into the salve bag and walked through the side door. As I approached the hole in the fence, there were two boys coming toward the factory shower room. When they saw me they turned and ran back down the road. I was puzzled for a moment until I realized that I must have looked like someone of authority in the coat and tie. I was pleased with myself.

I went to the Main Street Diner. I found a seat near the window where I would be able to see Mose Random's skeeterbug when it went by. Gloria Strong leaned over the table and asked in her angelic voice, "Hamburger, Coke and french fries?"

For some strange reason I said, "No. I'll have scrambled eggs, bacon and toast."

Gloria Strong noticed that I was wearing a coat and tie. She walked around in front of me and said in a low voice, "James Friend."

I turned from her stare and looked out the window.

I could see my father's reflection in the window of the diner as he opened the door. He stood scratching the side of his face for a minute and then ambled to one of the booths in the back of the diner. He sat with his back to me and I turned to make sure it was him. Gloria Strong brought him a cup of coffee. Although it was early afternoon, there were only three or four people in the diner. Gloria Strong sat reading her Bible by the cash register. She would read a line and then gaze off into the distance. She started to mumble a passage over and over. I could not make out the words. She stood with her hand on the Bible. Suddenly there was a high, shrill, piercing scream. "Jeeeeeeessssuuuuuss! Jeeeeeeessssuuuuuss!" Gloria was screaming the words at the top of her voice. She rushed to the shelves behind the cash register. She started throwing things through the window of the diner. There was a clashing sound as glass hit glass and shattered. Gloria was still screaming, "Jeeeeeeessssuuuuuss! Jeeeeeeessssuuuuuss!"

My father was saying, "Gloria, Gloria, Gloria. No! No! No!"

Gloria Strong ran from the diner, arms flailing, and turned, almost falling, into run-down Market Street to the Woodmont Coves First Methodist Church.

I got up and headed for the door. My legs were trembling so much that I could hardly walk. I managed to get to the sidewalk and hold on to the side of the building as I made my way down Main Street toward the dealership.

I sat with Mitch at the dealership. The Doctor Who Hated Fear drove up to the curb, jumped out and headed for the parking area. He asked me how I felt. I told him I felt fine now. The Thinking Man popped up to my left. He was holding the hand of The Singing

Girl. Jesus stood against the far wall wearing a long white robe. The Doctor Who Hated Fear said, "What can I do for you?"

I looked at all of them and said, "There is nothing I need." I clapped my hands and they began to disappear. I had clapped the last one away when I noticed that Mitch was clapping too. I held my hand toward him and he stopped clapping. He smiled at me, got to his feet and walked toward the shed for a bottle of wine.

Mose Random yelled at me from the street, "Hey, James, I've been looking for you. You know it's two thirty."

"Yeah."

"You goin'?"

"Yes. Wait a minute."

I gathered up my salve bag and ran to the skeeterbug. Mosey had a full load of pulpwood. "You got some more spending money here?" I asked.

"Yep. I figure we go first class tonight. Mo Jumpsum will be glad to see a couple of smooth-looking high rollers."

Mose Random was dressed in a white sports coat, pink shirt and a black tie. He reminded me of a rainbow, and I told him so. "I guess if we got right down to the end of you, we'd find a pot of gold."

"What's that?"

"I said if we got right down to the end of you, we'd find a pot of gold."

Mose Random laughed now. He looked at his shirt and tie and slapped me on the shoulder. "Ain't no danger'n you losin' me, is they?"

After we had hit the top of Hill Road and were

headed over the hill to Middletown, Mose reached into the back of the seat and pulled out a brown paper bag filled with cold cans of beer. My tie kept blowing into my face. I took it off and stuffed it inside my coat pocket.

The old man at the paper mill pounded on the pulp-wood with his hammer and called out, "Two passengers, no water."

Mose Random parked his skeeterbug alongside other similar vehicles and we walked across the parking lot and up the steep street to the small café where we had come the time before. "We meetin' the girls over at The Starlite Club about seven," Mosey said. "We might as well have us a couple of beers here before going over there."

Mose cashed his check and paid the girl a dollar for doing so. We drank beer and watched the Saturday afternoon crowd disperse, to be replaced by another group of better-dressed and better-spirited people.

The jukebox wailed out a song called "It's All Right to Cry":

> Way down deep in your heart
> You feel that last good-bye
> It's aaaaalllll riiigghhttt
> All right baby to cry

"That's Mo Jumpsum's new record. Ain't that something?" Mosey said. Mosey sang along;

> "It's aaaaaallllll riiiiggghhtttt!"

I noticed that the more beer Mosey drank the more

he let go of his grammar and pronunciation. I started imitating him.

"We gone be aw'rite tonite," I said to no one in particular.

It's all right baby to cryyyyyyyyyyyyyy!

Mose Random and I waited in the skeeterbug at The Starlite Club. We sat drinking beer from cans when a dark-blue car pulled into a parking space a few cars away from us. Mose jumped from the skeeterbug and said, "I think that's them now. Come on."

I walked along a few paces behind him. He shouted, "Hey Blondie, your lover-boy is here, ready and waitin'."

The two girls stood behind the car straightening their clothes and pushing their hair up with their hands. The blond-haired girl looked at me and asked, "You're James, ain't you?"

I said, "Yes."

"Well, this is Trina." She waved her hand at a small dark-haired girl. The girl stretched out her hand toward me and said, "Hi."

I said, "Hi."

Her handshake was very firm and quick. She wore a black pantsuit with a red sash around her waist. Her hair was rounded out in some sort of folded-under hair arrangement. It made her look altogether solid and compact. She wore a small gold cross on a thin gold chain around her neck. Her eyes seemed as dark as her attire. Her mouth was round, and her lips were painted dark red. Her round face and her slightly tilted nose gave her the appearance of a small rodent. Even with that, she was pleasant and moved solidly and confidently as we walked to the club.

Trina and I walked along behind a talkative and exuberant Mose Random. "We jump some with Jumpsum tonite, aw'rite." Mose Random finished the beer and threw the can under a parked car. We arrived at the ticket window of the club and Mose gave the man two five-dollar bills. He turned to me and said, "Five dollars apiece."

I reached into the salve bag and pulled out the small leather packet. I took a ten-dollar bill from it and laid it at the ticket window. Trina looked at my salve bag and looked at Blondie. "Is this man carrying a purse?" she wanted to know.

Mose Random stood bouncing to the music coming from inside. "Hey, ole James is all right. His old man's a doctor, and they all carry a bag of some kind, get it?" Mose laughed and opened the door to the club.

We stood in the foyer of the club for a few seconds until our eyes became accustomed to the dark interior. Although the foyer was small, the club widened out into a considerable expanse of tables and chairs. A waitress asked us if we would like to have dinner. Mose said, "No, thank you. We're here for the show."

A small railing separated the dinner-show crowd from the show-only crowd. We were escorted past the railing and led to a table with four chairs and a small candle burning inside a little clear glass vase on top.

A big man in an ill-fitting suit walked over to our table. He leaned toward me and pointed his finger at my neck. "You have to have a tie," he said in a very forceful way.

I took the tie from my pocket and clipped it onto the front of my shirt. The jukebox was playing more of Mo Jumpsum's records. I ordered a sloe gin over ice. Trina, the small, dark-haired girl, ordered a double scotch on the rocks. I grimaced when I heard her order. She smiled at my grimace and said, "Sloe gin will go well with your purse."

I leaned toward her and whispered, "I have a gun in this bag, and a knife, too. I'm gonna use 'em on you right after this show." I spoke very quietly and very deliberately. I smiled a cynical smile.

The dark-haired girl sat back and looked at me with curiosity. She took a sip of her drink and rummaged through her purse for a cigarette.

Mose Random and Blondie were dancing to almost every song. There was a small dance floor in front of the bandstand, and even though the band was just starting to set up, Mose and Blondie were dancing to the jukebox.

For a minute I didn't recognize the couple on the far side of the room. My view was blocked by the waiter who poured the wine and held the large menus. When he had moved and the light was better, I could see The Laughing Man and my mother sitting chatting over coffee and wine. The Laughing Man sipped a cup of coffee, and my mother held a wineglass in a lighthearted, conversational way. There were some papers on the table, and they seemed to be talking over some kind of a business deal. There was considerable shuffling of paperwork. I punched Mose Random's shoulder and said, "Isn't that The Laughing Man over there?"

Mose stood up and looked straight at the man and said, "By God, you're right, James. That is The Laughing Man."

I pulled Mose back into his seat and said, "Well, we won't bother him. I guess he's having dinner."

Since there was no chance that this evening with dark-haired Trina would amount to anything, I waited until Blondie and Mose were dancing and then left the club. My mother had not seen me in the dim light. It seemed ludicrous to see my mother and The Laughing Man together. I thought perhaps it was a joke that they were playing on me. I had hidden my drink under my coat, and I stood sipping it in the shadows cast by the awning of the club. As I stood there wondering what to do with myself, The Laughing Man came out of the club and walked past me to a large, luxurious automobile. He fished the keys from his pocket and opened the trunk. He leaned into the trunk of the car and opened a briefcase. I stepped away from the awning and into some shrubbery that fronted the building. The Laughing Man looked around to see if he was being watched. He removed a shiny bottle from the briefcase and took a long drink. He breathed deeply and then took another long drink. He replaced the bottle in the briefcase, put the briefcase back, locked the trunk of the car and marched back to the club. As he entered the club he saw me standing in the shrubbery and gave me a quizzical glance. I wondered why The Laughing Man was drinking from the trunk of his car when they sold all manner of drinks in the club.

I walked out into the parking lot and found Mose Random's old skeeterbug. It was a warm evening, and I removed my jacket, found a beer behind the seat and sat sipping it. I could hear the occasional burst of applause and the BOOM! BOOM! BOOM! of the music inside the club. I puzzled over the acquaintance of my mother and The Laughing Man.

 Dodd Givens replaced the windows at the Main Street Diner, and Gloria Strong prayed through on Saturday afternoon at the Woodmont Coves First Methodist Church. It was an unsettling experience for the town. Although she promised to pay for the broken windows, she was not apologetic about her experience. She seemed dreamily happy. And although the owners of the diner would have readily fired anyone so wrought up for any other reason, it could not be considered in light of the sacred premise of the afternoon's activities.

Dr. John Friend sat at his desk and wrote checks for bills that had accumulated in his wife's newfound life-style. Mrs. Buffet Friend had taken almost three thousand dollars in cash from their joint checking account. The lingerie bill from Goldman's Department Store surprised John Friend. He mused over the considerable bill and wondered about the meaning of such shopping. He noticed the flair with which his wife had signed the bill. Although Buffet Friend had a very neat signature, she had signed the bill with an almost indistinguishable scribble. John Friend finished writing the checks and placed them in their respective envelopes. He placed the envelopes at the edge of his desk where he would not forget to mail them.

John Friend was just beginning to realize how much work Buffet Friend had accomplished around the place. She had been receptionist, bookkeeper, cleaning lady, cook, gardener, and more. He wondered if there were something he should be doing that was not being done. He looked at the small desk that his wife had used and was frightened by the stacks of papers, forms and folders that he saw. Buffet Friend had gone about her work so quietly and efficiently that her husband had taken it all for granted. John Friend sat back at his desk and considered the possibility of a vacation; he dismissed the notion as foolish. He picked up the phone and dialed Van Alexander. He put his feet on his desk and leaned back in his chair as he hummed a small tune of unknown origin. Van Alexander came on the phone when his secretary buzzed him. "Alexander here."

"Van, this is John. How's the car business?"

"Oh, we sell a few and give some away. Are you buying or begging?"

"Listen, I've got an idea. We used to catch some pretty good bass out of Boo River, didn't we?"

"Yeah, we did."

"Let's go fishing."

Van Alexander was sure he had heard John Friend right, but he repeated the idea. "Go fishing?"

"Yes, just hang a sign out that says 'Gone fishing.'"

Van Alexander was silent for a few seconds. Then he spoke into the phone in a quiet voice. "Doc, you want to fish or talk?"

John Friend laughed. "Well, uh, both. Yes, we'll fish and talk. I'll meet you over there at ole Minner's Dick in about thirty minutes. I've got some poles here some-place, and I'll bring the bait."

Van Alexander laughed into the phone. "Hey, John, you're not taking your own dope, are you?"

John Friend said, "I'll meet you there."

Rummaging around in a closet, John Friend found two old fishing rods and reels. There was an old tackle box sitting on the floor of the closet, and he picked it up, too, not even bothering to look inside.

Dodd Givens handed John Friend a small mattock and told him not to remove the price tag. He shouted after John Friend as he left the hardware store, "You ought to buy that mattock and donate it to the city. Everybody uses it anyway."

John Friend walked across behind Strong's Supermarket and was disappointed to see that the recent flood had washed away most of the good worm-digging debris that usually lay behind the market. He picked up a few old boards and some recent boxes and found several big red wiggly worms. He put them into a small can and returned the mattock to Dodd Givens.

John Friend enjoyed the short walk along the banks of the Boo River. He remembered this stream well from his childhood. His family had moved from Woodmont Coves when he was eleven years old, and John Friend had returned for the simple reasons that his father owned a house here and he needed a place to practice his medicine. He approached Minner's Dick, a long, slick rock that he remembered from childhood. It looked small and insignificant. He remembered that he and Van Alexander had slid down the rock and dove into the river for a swim. It was not a rock that needed a name, he thought. It was so small that he was surprised both of them remembered it after more than thirty years. He stood considering the rock when he heard Van Alexander's voice. "Don't catch 'em all, John. I'm coming."

John Friend looked around to see Van Alexander approaching him. He was dressed in a silvery-gray suit, soft white shirt, and a silver-and-brown tie. John Friend regretted some of his joviality when he saw the tall, neat figure of his friend picking his way among the weeds and rocks. He thought it might be too soon after the recent tragedy involving his friend's son's sentencing to life imprisonment.

Van Alexander stood on the banks of the Boo River and stretched while taking a long, deep breath. "I haven't been over here in years. It's funny how you live so near a thing and never see it. Well, they say there are people in Cincinnati who have never been to the zoo."

John Friend had taken a seat on a long log that stretched along the riverbank. "Have a seat, Van. I've found a couple of hooks in this tackle box, and I've got the bait. Want to make a bet on who'll catch the biggest fish?"

"Now, John, you know you can catch fish better than I can. You said it was in the chemistry of the body. Some fish like certain people."

"I still maintain that, by the way."

John Friend and Van Alexander sat quietly for a few minutes, watching the lines of their fishing poles hang listlessly in the water.

John Friend said, "I'm just going to say one more time that I hate what happened to Willie."

Van Alexander reeled his line in a little and said, "You know, John, I appreciate that, but if you want to do some talking I'll tell you that I'm not that sorry about it. Oh, I miss Willie, and I never minded him, really. I mean, who gives a shit how he lived. When my wife died I had pretty much the same emotions. I thought I'd at least have freedom. Then, when I realized how much I really loved her, I hated myself for considering the freedom. And then I got over the guilt and realized that I didn't want or, for that matter, *need* freedom. You know what I mean?"

"I think I know exactly what you mean."

John Friend was interrupted as he started to say something else. Someone yelled to him from downriver, "Dr. Friend, Dr. Friend!" It was one of the girls from the pharmacy.

John Friend hollered back, "What is it?"

The girl from the pharmacy stood downstream at the edge of the river. She said, "Mrs. Lowe wants to know if she can refill her prescription?"

John Friend hollered again, "Yes, yes, it's okay."

The young girl shouted a thank you and went back toward the pharmacy.

Van Alexander asked, "What's Mrs. Lowe taking?"

John Friend thought for a minute and said, "I don't know. Buffet must have called it in."

Van Alexander gave a hard jerk on the line of his pole. "Hey, I almost got him that time."

He pulled the line from the water and put another worm on the hook. He looked at John Friend and said, "John, is Buffet coming back?"

John Friend scratched his chin and said, "I don't know, Van, I really don't know what her plans are. Have you seen her lately?"

"No, I haven't."

"Well, she's lost about thirty pounds and bought a whole new wardrobe. She still looks like a middle-aged woman to me, but she thinks she's nineteen again. I don't know if it's menopause or not. She's made some dramatic changes in her looks and personality. I'm still waiting for her to sort things out."

Van Alexander said, "Waiting for things to regulate themselves?"

John Friend smiled and said, "Yep, still waiting for regulation."

Van Alexander laid his pole aside and lit a cigarette. He blew the smoke into the still summer afternoon and said, "John, what's happening to all of us? Is it just that time of our lives? Is this the normal way things are supposed to start crumbling at this age?"

John Friend spoke. "You know, there's something to that, Van. What's that quote about 'Whom the gods would destroy they first make mad'? Is that what it was? Maybe we are not doing the wrong things. I don't know how all of what's happened here of late can be explained. It all seems so disconnected. Do you suppose there is some central mysterious figure tying it all together around here?"

"Human nature," Van Alexander said.

John Friend continued. "You know, you can't fix things. I mean, you can't regulate life. Willie's being a homosexual doesn't matter. Buffet wanting to start her life over doesn't matter. Oh, it matters to me because I would rather have the convenience of her work and the social comfort of having a wife. It doesn't matter that James is a freethinker, and it doesn't matter that he does as he pleases. I guess Buffet was his biggest problem. She wanted him to be a more conventional son, a more distant success. By that I mean he should have succeeded at some distant point away from her having to drag him around socially. Women are embarrassed by grown children. It's not as if life were being held in abeyance; life goes on and things *do* regulate themselves. It's when we try to correct things immediately that we make mistakes. Maude Primm tried to help, I'm sure of it. Willie would not have run from an understanding policeman. Joe Morgan would not have killed a more generous Claudia Barnes. Claudia Barnes would not have threatened a more considerate Joe Morgan. We simply make too much of what we have and who we think we are. Vanity and greed are the key words of the problem—and time is the answer. It has to be."

Van Alexander shook his head in agreement and said, "I rattle around that old house of mine more than ever now. I cleaned out the den and had them paint the walls. We found a lot of electrical and plastic apparatus in there for sex. Are you aware of all the junk you can order through the mail?"

"I'm aware of it. There are more things produced to

please the human senses than all other industries in the world put together. Automobiles are designed to that end, if you want to be exact about it."

"I guess so."

John Friend shifted his weight and said, "Well, all of this heavy talking must be scaring the fish away."

Van Alexander reeled his line in a little ways. "Sometimes I think it would be a good idea to just drop a bomb on this town and forget it."

John Friend thought of his pistol lying beside his chair at home. "Yes, it would at least be a good idea to threaten them with it once a day."

Van Alexander laughed. "Yeah, just circle the town every afternoon and say, 'One peep out of you folks and B O O M!'"

Van Alexander went back to his car at Strong's Supermarket and drove back to his dealership. He parked in his reserved parking space and entered through the side door to his office. Even though it was still daylight, he flipped on the light switch to brighten the atmosphere. Buffet Friend said, "Hello, Van."

Van Alexander was startled and turned quickly to see Buffet Friend sitting in one of the soft leather chairs with her purse in her lap. He walked over to her at once and embraced and kissed her. "You shouldn't be here, not now, not so soon."

"Well, I'm here. Did you tell him?"

"I couldn't do it, Buff. The old son of a bitch is sitting down there fishing and philosophizing. He has no earthly idea that we even know one another that well."

Buffet Friend stood and walked over to the window. She spoke. "Van, you've killed a man—a cop. You've put your son in prison, and you've done it all for me. Do you mean to tell me that you can't face John and tell him about us?"

Van Alexander grew angry, almost shouting, "Buff, I thought the world of Jimmy Barrett. I just couldn't be seen coming out of your house at eleven thirty at night. It don't matter about Willie. I think he looked forward to living with men." Van Alexander stood and rubbed his forehead while he walked around the room. "Ain't that strange. It seems like he liked the idea. If he had been straight and had not been on drugs, he could have beaten that charge. You know, when he came to me and told me he killed Jimmy Barrett I nearly fainted. I thought he knew about me. I swear I think he almost believed it himself. I just figured he wanted to be in prison. I thought he'd jump and scream when the prosecution mentioned execution. My head is killing me."

Buffet Friend came over to Van Alexander and took his head in her hands. "Van, we have what we both want now. I have the house and you have me. I think John will understand. He's going to blow his damned brains out one day anyway. I just don't want to wait any longer. Look what I've done for you, Van. I've nearly killed myself to be your idea of a woman. You love me, don't you?"

Van Alexander took her into his arms and nestled his chin in her hair. "I've always loved you, Buff. None of this is as hard as telling John about it. I don't believe I'll ever be able to just say it out loud to him."

Van Alexander moved across the room and sat at his desk. "I think some people are suspicious about redecorating so soon. The decorator keeps mentioning a Mrs. Alexander, and most of these local painters and carpenters know better. I explained to one that he's talking about my mother, but you'd better mention it to him."

Van Alexander held his hands in front of him and looked at his palms. "I can't believe what these hands have done in the past three weeks. I wanted my life to be neat. I really wanted it to be right and orderly. Look at us standing here talking as if we'd been to a picnic. Who saw you come in here?"

"Everybody saw me come in here. I'm having some tires put on John's old car. I swear he got them five or six years ago. I told them I wanted to use your phone to make some calls."

Van Alexander pushed the intercom on his phone. "Is Mrs. Al . . . Friend's car ready yet?"

There was a clicking sound on the intercom and a lady's voice said, "It's about ready. We're working on the billing. Where would she like it sent?"

"Where you've always sent it, I guess." Van Alexander tried to sound casual.

"Buff, you've got to get out of here and let this thing cool down for a few days. How are you doing in Middletown?"

"I'm still working with the religious crusade. It's one of the most challenging things I've done outside the church."

"You're working in a crusade and you're standing here taking part in all of this. What kind of pill did you give me that night at your house? Are you taking that? I swear I barely remember seeing Jimmy Barrett."

"I'm not taking any pills—not an aspirin, not a cold tablet, nothing!"

"Bullshit."

"No, really Van. I thought you wanted to make love. I just gave you something to get you excited. I didn't know you were that nervous about being in the house."

"Make love in your house? John was barely six blocks away drinking coffee. He could have walked in at any minute."

"That's the point about you and me, Van. John sits all night listening to tapes about constipation and venereal disease; you care about clothes, music, travel and life."

Mose Random and I arrived back in Woodmont Coves at odds with one another. The two girls had abandoned Mose and had left the club with two of Mo Jumpsum's musicians. Mose blamed me for making the dark-haired girl angry and for busting up his evening's plans. I had been waiting in the skeeterbug when Mose came out of the club. I had to put up with his ranting and raving all the way back to Woodmont Coves. "Man, I don't get it. I've got these chicks lined up and programed for a great Saturday night. What does 'the marine' do? He gets up and sits in a skeeterbug all night drinking beer and counting stars. I could have brought a dog with me for company. At least it wouldn't have pissed off the prettiest girl in Middletown." There was more. "Singing? Huh, I can hear singing anywhere. I can even sing myself. I went there to that club to get them girls excited and ready for fun. Dancing? Huh, I can dance by myself. Get it? I can tap dance, ballet, shuffle and—you know what I mean? I was trying to get you some poontang. I was being your buddy, I was being your pal. I could have brought a dog. Trina likes dogs." It went on and on.

Finally I said, "You know, Mose, life is full of strange twists and turns. It never seems to settle down and rest. Things change every day. Have you ever noticed that? When the sun is shining and things are going good and the fish are biting and the weather is just like being indoors—warm, I mean—then BOOM! A nut or bolt comes loose in something and you're sitting there with all the pieces in your hand, but you can't remember what you did with the thing when it was all together. You're always wondering why you didn't say or do this or that when you had the chance yesterday, when it really would have helped. At the time those things should be done it seems like we're off doing something else. You know what I mean?"

Mose and I were pretty drunk. Mose looked at me sideways and almost ran off the road. The wheels of the skeeterbug dug into the loose gravel on the shoulder of the road and the car righted itself, just avoiding slamming into the bushes. Mose settled into his seat a little more firmly and pretended the narrow escape had not occurred. He slowed the vehicle by about ten miles per hour and spoke. "You know you got something there."

"My aunt is like you say, James, always wondering what's gonna happen next. She keeps track of all kinds of relatives I don't even know. She keeps saying how sorry they must be for not having been kinder to this dead one or that dead one after they're gone. She don't feel too guilty herself, but she sure likes to make the rest of 'em feel bad. I asked her the other day how she figured she was gonna make something right today that was wrong yesterday. See? 'They wouldn't a done that when Ben was alive'—she says things like that. I say, if you get to aggravating yourself, get out and get busy. I've been down. I know the feeling. I just get out and cut up about two loads of wood and pretty soon I'm more worried about something to eat than I am about old Ben and a bunch of dead yesterdays. Hey, that's pretty good, ain't it? I mean, you know, for a song?" Mose sang it:

> "Deeeeeaaaaddd yeeeessstttteeerrddaayyysss
> Woo dat   woo dat
> Deeeeeaaaaddd yeeeessstttteeerrddaayyysss"

Mose's joviality did not last long. He was soon back to haranguing me for not being easier to get along with in female company. We were back to driving fast and shouting over the rattling old skeeterbug. We pulled to the side of the road when Mose announced that he needed to "water the flowers."

We were a little startled when Bill Lovette, the newly appointed police chief and brother of Mayor Arthur Lovette, walked up beside the skeeterbug. "Hello, boys. How's everything going? Having a little fun, I reckon?"

Mose swung around and urinated on Bill Lovette's boots. He quickly zipped up his pants and spoke as casually as he could. "Oh, yeah, we were just relieving ourselves a little. Nice night, ain't it?"

Bill Lovette pulled his pants up over his bulging

stomach and continued in his casual tone. "Been kind of a quiet Saturday night around here. You got a driver's licence? I'd like to see it just as a routine matter. I love these summer nights. Reminds me of when I was a young feller." The police chief rubbed his big, round, scraggly-looking face and pushed his hat back over his graying, rumpled hair.

Mose Random handed his wallet, containing his driver's license, to the chief of police and stood waiting for him to examine it with his flashlight. The chief handed the wallet back to Mose and said, "Would you take the license out, please?" Mose took the license out and handed it to the chief. The chief said, "You have a permit to drive this skeeterbug? You been hauling wood, ain't you?" Mose nodded his head that he had been doing so. The chief said, "Well, you need a permit for hauling wood. It's only a couple of bucks. Why don't you boys follow me down to the station. We'll get Mr. Random a permit and everything will be fine."

Mose Random reached for his driver's license, but Bill Lovette tucked it into his shirt pocket and said, "Just follow me. I sure love these summer nights. Makes me wish I was a young boy again. Just follow me, boys."

We traveled slowly down Hill Avenue behind the police car. Mose said, "Now, if all police guys were like that, this'd be a better place to live. If that'd been Jimmy Barrett, he'd a locked us up in a minute."

We walked into the lighted front area of the police station and waited while Bill Lovette opened a door at the back of the room. He motioned for Mose Random to follow him. Although I could not see them, I could hear Mose saying that he'd be glad to wait out front with me while the chief filled out the permit. I heard a clanging sound as a cell door closed. Bill Lovette came back into the room where I was and said, "You better go on home, James. Mr. Random is gonna be with us for a while."

It took my father three days to talk the people at the jail into letting Random go. It cost Mose $186.50 and a suspended thirty-day jail term. He had to report to Chief Lovette every Friday afternoon for four weeks.

Blondie drove by the dealership one afternoon and asked me if I had seen Mose. I told her I had not. She looked up and down the streets for a few minutes and said, "I ain't seen him in over three weeks. Is he all right, you think?"

"Oh, I think he's okay," I said. Trina, the dark-haired girl, stared straight ahead as they drove off down the street.

 The Laughing Man stood before the long mirror with stained-oak borders and admired his new tailor-made blue suit. He adjusted the red-and-blue striped tie and turned ever so slightly to get a look at his profile. He smiled broadly and noted that he had lost a few pounds. Either that or the blue suit made him look less heavy. The tailor stood behind him with a pleased look and occasionally smoothed a wrinkle or gave an approving nod. The Laughing Man strolled around the exclusive, well-decorated shop for a minute and then

came back to the mirror. He raised his hands in a sort of double military salute and shouted "Glory! Glory! Glory!"

The startled tailor stood wide-eyed behind him. The Laughing Man turned to him with a wide smile. "I'll take them all, sir. I'll take them all. Glory!"

The tailor made a gesture of small applause and turned to start the billing for six dark-blue suits, fifteen pale-blue shirts, and three red-and-blue striped ties. The Laughing Man turned to the lady sitting on a gold velour stool and said, "What do you think? Okay?"

Buffet Friend checked off something in her notebook and said, "On the money. Perfect!"

Dr. John Friend wrote his letter:

Dear Buffet,

I had meant to dispense with courtesies, but I do hope this letter finds you well and happy.

I know about you and Van. I really don't disapprove; it wouldn't make any difference if I did. I hope your lawyers will remember that Van has more money than I have—or will ever have. I could counter with alienation of affection, but I don't want to do that. The nights you thought I was listening to tapes I was actually making some. I have some conversations between you and Van, to be exact. I also think there is something strange about Jimmy Barrett's death. I can't put my finger on it, but I have my doubts that it was as assumed.

I might specialize when I get to Cincinnati. There's room for it. I'm bringing another fella into this practice. I would like to sell what I have here, including the house, if your lawyers can understand that. I won't have to ask anything for the practice, which would be unethical; I could just throw that into the price of the real estate. From the conversations I've heard, I don't believe you like this house anyway.

I took Van fishing to give him an opportunity to talk, but he just fished and stared into the water.

Since you'll be here, I wish you could keep an eye on James. He seems settled here of late.

By the time you have redecorated your new house, I'll be gone. I'll have to stay until these folks have confidence in the new man. He's an M.D. and a psychiatrist. He should have fun here.

Best of luck,

John

The young man tacked the poster onto the utility pole and stood back to admire his work. It was a huge poster of a stern-looking Laughing Man. He was dressed in a dark suit and a striped tie. The poster contained the caption:

WOODMONT COVES HIGH SCHOOL GYM
FRIDAY NIGHT, 7:30 P.M.
Free Admission
First Come First Served

The young man wondered why The Laughing Man's name did not appear on the poster. He shrugged his shoulders and threw the hammer into the pickup truck and went about his work.

Maude Primm and Gloria Strong sat at the small kitchen table in Maude Primm's apartment and discussed two books. One was the Bible and the other was a pharmaceutical directory of drugs. Maude Primm talked as Gloria Strong flipped through the pages of colorful pills, tablets, and capsules. "I never take amphetamines anymore. There are so many good, new drugs on the market. They change every few months, discovering this and that. The best high is a small pain pill with a little tranquilizer thrown in. A coffee now and then or a glass of wine will keep you going real well. Don't you worry about paying for them. I've got us fixed for life." She took a small stack of mail from a cupboard and handed Gloria Strong a small package. "See what's in there?"

Gloria laid the package aside and said, "Do you think the Lord meant for us to take pills, Maude?"

"I say, if it was put here to help us, then we should help ourselves to it. Do you know that most of the people in this town depend on one drug or another?"

"Really?"

"How's this for a for instance. Mrs. John Friend has been on drugs since she got to this town."

"Have you seen her? She must have lost thirty pounds."

"She's after Van Alexander. Did you know?"

"Mrs. Friend and Mr. Alexander? Are you kidding?"

"Honey, it would make your hair stand on end to know the real story of this town."

"Maude, do you think I could be called to the ministry? I mean, I think the Lord works through women as well as men. Sex is what I'm talking about. I hate to say that, but it might hold me back from the Lord's work."

"Listen, honey, you wait 'til Friday night and see how these organized revivals work. They got more show business than anything you've ever seen. When you hit the backstage of the place for your preparation prayer, you'll hear how the devil works for the Lord. Did you know that they asked me for ten dollars to cover the cost of my choir robe? Me? I'm taking up collection and singing in the choir to boot, and they want ten dollars from me!"

"I gave them ten dollars. I think it's such an honor to be able to sing with such a great group."

"Well, you'll be on the back row, and you won't be on the speakers. They try to convince people that these choirs are part of the traveling show. In fact, the front row will be doing the driving, nailing up posters, and setting up the stage before this show gets under way."

"I wish you wouldn't call it a show. That sounds so cruel."

"I've got my religion, Gloria. The Lord has given me the light to see above and below and around things in this world. I don't intend to let some religious shyster alter my faith in the least. God forgive me."

Maude went to the freezer and looked inside. "You want a hamburger? I'm hungry as all get-out."

Gloria held her palm out in disgust. "If I ever see another hamburger, I'll scream."

Maude Primm threw the hamburger back into the freezer and asked, "How 'bout a bowl of hot chicken noodle soup? It'll bring you down, but I make it good."

"Soup sounds just fine," Gloria said. "By the way, you ought to air out your freezer; it's got a musty smell."

Friday morning I sat inside my trailer and watched it rain. Little streams of water would trickle down the small window, and I would try to guess where the stream would reach the bottom sill. I was right five out of ten times. Once in a while the wind would mix the little streams all together and I would change my guesses.

When the wind came gusting against my window, changing the streams, the picture outside would change into a blur. After one such gust I watched the picture change into a misty but discernible scene. The Singing Girl was swinging and singing:

"Words Words Words Words Words Words"

I stepped from the trailer and walked to where I could see her better. Even though she was swinging in the rain, she was completely dry. She stopped her singing and looked at me. She smiled at me and displayed a beautiful row of sparkling white teeth. She kept swinging and spoke to me. "The Doctor Who Hated Fear fixed my teeth. Nice, huh?"

I stood with my hands in my pockets and my collar turned up against the wind. "I don't care anymore. About you or any of them. It doesn't matter. You can't harm me. You have no bearing on my disposition. No fear of you. No fear."

"Oh, smarty-pants. Have you found another song you like better than mine?"

"No."

"Well, I still got your favorite song" she replied, and sang:

"Words Words Words Words Words Words"

"Do you know 'It's All Right to Cry'?"

"Of course not," The Singing Girl said exasperated. "Why should I know such a song?"

"It's a better song than 'Words'." I fell to my knees and started to laugh. I clapped my hands together and laughed. I pounded my fist against the ground and laughed.

The old lady who ran the trailer park was suddenly standing above me with an umbrella. "Mercy me, what now?"

I got to my feet and looked at her. "Just practicing for The Laughing Man Show."

I went back inside the trailer and gathered my things for a shower at the paint factory.

When I made my way into the paint factory showers, I found The Thinking Man sitting on one of the redwood benches. I threw my salve bag down on the bench beside him and said, "Well, what's the big idea today?" I slapped him on the knee as I spoke.

The Thinking Man laughed and said, "Nothing new under the sun—and no sun, for that matter."

"You're right. It's raining harder than ever now. How do you keep all those white clothes so clean?"

"No bother at all for a man who is an incarnation."

"Well, of course," I said mockingly.

"Been doing any thinking?"

"Nope."

"None at all?"

"Nope."

"Good. It makes you tired, doesn't it?"

"Nope."

"Going to see The Laughing Man tonight?"

"That's what I'm getting all cleaned up for. Have never missed The Laughing Man Show, not since I was a little boy."

The Thinking Man got up and walked around the room touching one thing and then another. "The paint odor is terrible around here."

I turned and looked at him. "Is it? I've been coming here so long I didn't even notice it."

"That's my whole point. One doesn't notice something after a while. Things sort of disappear from one's understanding when they disappear from one's notice. See that avenue of thought? There are millions of things around us that we never notice. Therefore they do not exist. It's part of the evolutionary process."

"And how does that involve me?"

"You take better notice, that's all. I thought you might like to know that."

"Well, I don't."

"Very well. I'll see you tonight."

"You're coming to The Laughing Man Show?"

"I go where you go. I'm part of your universe."

"Do you have a raincoat?"

"No, I don't *think* it's raining now. Get it? I don't *think* it's raining now."

"Ha, ha, ha, sure. Hey, that's okay. Take care."

The Thinking Man disappeared. I stacked my clothes on the bench and stepped into the hot, clean, refreshing water. I could smell the paint.

Maude Primm had told Gloria Strong to go ahead and cry it all out. She had burst into tears while reading the Bible. Maude said, "Cry it all out, child; it'll do you good. I'm out of chicken noodle soup. I'll run across the street and get some. You must pray it all out and you'll feel better."

Maude grabbed an old raincoat and threw it across her shoulders. She went down the apartment steps. She noticed that the door at the bottom of the steps was still open and that the rain blew in. The door had been open since she could remember; no one ever thought of closing it. She tried the door to see if it would close and spotted an iron behind the door. Maude Primm shuddered as she remembered how it had gotten there. She thought back to when she had seared the palms of Dr. Friedman's hands. She picked up the iron and noticed that there were dried bits of something stuck to the bottom. She scraped off the bits against the third step of the stair and set the iron there to be taken back to the apartment.

Although it was only a block and a half to Strong's Supermarket, Maude Primm thought it would be best if she took the car. It was parked in front of the building and the rain was pouring down.

It was unavoidable. Lightning struck something near

the side of the road, and Maude Primm's car swung into another shocked driver as the two cars collided in front of the supermarket. It was an hour and a half before Bill Lovette filled out the forms and asked all the questions. The cars had to be towed away, both front ends and wheels having been smashed. Maude Primm sat in Strong's Supermarket talking to Lydia Strong and drinking coffee. "My goodness," she said, "I was supposed to take Gloria some chicken noodle soup."

"How can you think of chicken noodle soup at a time like this? You could have been killed."

Maude Primm rubbed her forehead and laughed. "I'm not hurt, Lydia. All we did was bend a few fenders. I've been gone for two hours or more. Gloria must think I've left the country."

Maude Primm selected two cans of chicken noodle soup for which Lydia refused payment. She picked up her raincoat and walked the block and a half back to her apartment. She was having a hard time sorting out reality as a result of the pills she had been taking before the accident.

Maude Primm found Gloria Strong lying face down in the middle of the apartment. The floor was covered with excretion. Maude Primm dragged the body to a clean part of the room. She wiped the mouth of Gloria Strong. There were bottles and packages of medicine all over the place. Maude Primm guessed that Gloria Strong had taken several kinds of pills and capsules. Maude Primm picked up two of the pills she recognized and chased them down with a glass of water. She sat on the edge of the chair and considered the situation at hand. "This will put an end to my private pharmacy when this gets out," she thought. "Why has the Lord visited this upon me? Gloria, Gloria. You had so much to live for. You were just beginning to get hold of yourself and grow up, and in the arms of the Lord."

Such were the thoughts of Maude Primm as she picked up the limp body and moved toward the freezer. She placed Gloria Strong's body in the freezer in a sitting position. The lid would not close; Gloria was too tall. Maude Primm put her hand behind the head of the body and pressed the head toward the knees. She closed the lid.

It took a short time to clean up the mess on the floor and to gather the pills and capsules. Gloria Strong's purse lay on the table. Maude Primm picked it up and threw it into the freezer with the body. She was perspiring after all the fury of the afternoon.

Maude Primm rehearsed the speech that she would make to Lydia Strong after the crusade had left town:

"Lydia, Gloria wanted to work for the Lord. You know how proud you were when she joined the church and prayed through. Well, this is what she wanted. She's a big girl now. She can handle herself. It's not as if she were a cheerleader, you know, with boys chasing her and all that. She is a dedicated Christian now, and she deserves a chance to work it out on her own. She'll be fine. She told me to tell you that she would write to you as soon as she is settled; she said not to worry about a thing. The crusade will be on the road a few more weeks and then she'll get settled and write to you so you can keep in touch. The people at the crusade were so impressed with her devotion to the Lord. Why, they said she was one of the finest workers they could hope to find. You know, she could have done a lot worse than join up with a crusade for the Lord."

Maude Primm considered the speech a good one. She would, after that speech, refuse to know anything more. Maude Primm opened the two cans of chicken noodle soup and placed them in a small pan on the stove. She would have to start getting ready to sing in the choir tonight.

As the pills began to take effect, Maude Primm sat and stared at the freezer. She was surprised when the lid raised itself and Gloria Strong crawled from the freezer and looked around bewildered. "My God, Maude, I'm freezing to death. I tried to take a pill *dry* and almost strangled. I think I'll just take a small nap."

Gloria Strong walked unsteadily and shivering toward the bed and collapsed with a deep, childish sigh.

Maude Primm sipped her hot soup. "I'll wake you in time to get dressed for the crusade, honey."

People were hushed as Mitch and I made our way through the side door and took our seats under the bleachers. Mitch was in a particularly good mood. He sat bouncing beside me and rambled along with an almost inaudible monologue.

Suddenly the lights went out. The blackness lasted for a second or two. And then we heard the loud voices of singers. It startled Mitch and me so much we jumped and banged our heads on the bleacher seats. The music was from an organ, and the voices were strong and loud:

"WORDS, WORDS, WORDS, WORDS, WORDS, WORDS"

I looked at Mitch as the lights beamed toward the larger-than-usual stage. There were swirling and flashing lights that didn't settle on any particular object long enough to identify anything or anybody.

The music and the singing grew softer and softer. Reverend Bill Turner could be seen on the stage now. He was introducing Mayor Arthur Lovette to the crowd. There was some confusion as Reverend Turner tried to adjust the microphone for the shorter Mayor Lovette. I could hear the sound of the voice, but it seemed to be coming from some high, echoing place. I saw my mother standing to the right of Arthur Lovette. She wore a bright-blue floor-length gown. There was a flower of some kind pinned to the front of her dress. She held a huge white Bible. Arthur Lovette nervously stumbled through his speech. There was a loud choral response following the introduction of someone. The lights were made to swirl and sway again. The Laughing Man strode from the wings of the stage with an intensity that I could not fathom. He walked to my mother and was presented with the Bible she had been holding. There was another tremendous choral response to this ceremony. The Laughing Man stood before the microphone mumbling an inaudible prayer before he burst into his speech:

"I AM HERE TONIGHT TO BRING YOU A MESSAGE OF SALVATION. [Mitch leaves the building] I AM HERE TO BRING A MESSAGE OF HOPE [Pause] AND [Pause] LOVE. [Choral response] I KNOW YOU CAME TO SEE THE LAUGHING MAN [Pause] WELL, TONIGHT YOU ARE GOING TO SEE THE PREACHING MAN. [Small burst of laughter from the choir] JESUS IS HERE TONIGHT! [I look around the room, but He is not here] JESUS HAS A MESSAGE FOR YOU. I HAVE BEEN CHOSEN TO BRING YOU THAT MESSAGE. MANY ARE CALLED, BUT FEW ARE CHOSEN. I BELIEVE THAT I WAS CHOSEN TO BRING YOU THIS MESSAGE. [Murmurings of "Amen"] TEN WEEKS AGO I WAS ASLEEP IN MY HOME IN MIDDLETOWN. A FIRE WAS RAGING THROUGH MY BEDROOM. I ESCAPED WITH MY LIFE BECAUSE GO-AHD HAD SOMETHING FOR ME TO DO. YOU KNOW THAT STORY. IT WAS IN ALL THE PAPERS. WELL [Pause] I'VE COME HERE TONIGHT TO TELL YOU *THE GREATEST STORY.* [Choral response] JESUS DIED FOR YOUR SINS. HE DIED FOR MY SINS. WE HAVE ALL SINNED AND COME SHORT OF THE GLORY OF GO-AHD. [Weeping in the choir] I WANT TO SPEAK ABOUT THE BIBLE. I WANT TO PREACH FROM THE BOOK. [Pauses to wipe

perspiration from brow] HOW MUCH LAUGH-
ING DO YOU FIND IN THE BIBLE?
THINK ABOUT IT. THE BIBLE IS A
BOOK OF DEAD SERIOUSNESS. THE
BIBLE IS NOT A BOOK OF HUMOR!
THERE IS NO HUMOR IN THE BIBLE.
NO HUMOR. DID YOU HEAR ME? NO
HUMOR IN THE BIBLE. WHAT IN GO-
AHD'S NAME WERE WE LAUGHING
ABOUT? [Two dozen people leave the building]
WE WERE LAUGHING OUR WAY TO
HELL [Pause] THAT'S WHAT WE WERE
DOING. [Gloria Strong weeps openly and is com-
forted by Maude Primm] JESUS IS HERE
TONIGHT. [I get to my feet and start toward the
stage. I am wearing my iron shoes on my square
feet. My head is like a block of steel. I am muscular
and strong.] NO HUMOR IN THERE AT
ALL, MY FRIENDS." [I walk to where the
Laughing/Preaching Man is standing and gently
take the microphone from his hand. He is confused
and thinks I am one of the sound technicians. I walk
to the center of the stage and make my speech.]

"We cannot stop the laughter. We can't do without the laughter. Laughter keeps us happy. Don't
you know that? Why not have a little laughing here?
Let's all do "The Laughing Song" now. I know you
can laugh. We've done this before. Don't be afraid
of all the robes and lights and mournful talking.
Let's all laugh a good laugh right now. How 'bout
it, huh?"

My mother, Gloria, Maude, and Bill Lovette came and took me by the arm. I was led from the stage as I tried to coax the audience into laughing. I was happy. I was speechless. My hearing deserted me; consequently I could not hear the crying of my mother or the admonitions of Gloria Strong. A great peace came over me, as if I had found some great, quiet secret.

I was taken to the Middletown Mental Health Center, where I now reside.

The last time I saw Woodmont Coves it was cold and snowing. I stood with The Thinking Man and looked down into the little valley from atop a high hill. I thought of many things at once, many, many things at once:

    watches
    razor blades
    blue lights
    shotguns
    pies
    dresses
    paint
    knives
    gold stars
    deer
    sloe gin
    wine
    shoes
    rabbits
    pills

caskets
flowers
fish
worms
trees
trucks
girls
water
freezers
sunshine
hammering
sawing
singing
fear
vomit
books
letters
crying
LAUGHING
praying
monologues
chicken noodle soup
brandy
sleep

The Thinking Man stood with his hands in the pockets of his white coat and seemed sad and dejected. I turned to him and said, "Was it a thing you *had* to do?"

The Thinking Man said, "Yes."

"It's a nice town."

"The people are, and were, nice. Towns, bah." He kicked the dirty snow with his foot. "There's a town," he said. And then he pointed to a tree. "There's a town. Towns are here and there and everywhere. Towns are nothing, absolutely nothing; but people, ah, now there it is."

"I disagree."

"Of course you do. You don't have to live here anymore."

"You'll stay?"

The Thinking Man looked at me quizzically. "Of course I'll stay. Where would I go?"

"Almost anywhere, I would think."

"Who will deliver me from earth?"

"Can't you do that?"

"No, I'll be here. Someone will come along who has need of me."

"My father is a wise man."

"And therefore has no need of me."

"Yes, I see."

The Thinking Man scuffed his feet in the snow and looked longingly at the gray winter sky. "You know something?"

"What?"

"I don't like white."

"No?"

"No, I really don't. But there's the contest, you know?"

"Contest?"

"Good and evil—that contest."

"Oh yes, of course."

As I finish writing this story here at the Middletown Mental Health Center, if I have not already told you, there are trees around the place. There are small benches scattered among the trees. Sometimes we can go there and sit and wonder. I can see people out there around the trees now. The Laughing Man is listening intently to The Thinking Man. The Singing Girl is entertaining The Doctor Who Hated Fear. Jesus sits quietly, away from the others, reading His Father's Biography.

There are two men standing looking at me through a plate-glass window. I can't hear them. Their moving lips tell me that they are talking about me. One says to the other, "Who is that?" The other replies, "We call him The Laughing Man of Woodmont Coves."

Thank you.